BEHIND THE PICKET FENCE

BEHIND

THE

PICKET

FENCE

KORI JANE SPAULDING

For Mom, Dad, Cade, Hallie and Lacey.

"The gods envy us. They envy us because we're mortal, because any moment may be our last. Everything is more beautiful because we're doomed. You will never be lovelier than you are now. We will never be here again."

—HOMER, THE ILIAD

CONTENTS

Dramatis Personae

Alissa [*uh*-lis-*uh*]: *wanderer*

Bella [bel-*uh*]: *beautiful one*

Blaire [blair]: *plain*

Brennan [bren-*uh*n]: *sorrow* or *teardrop*

Caleb [kay-lu*h*b]: *bold* or *brave*

Camille [k*uh*-meel]: *perfect* or *helper*

Cobalt [koh-bawlt]: *element on periodic table*

Dillon [dil-*uh*n]: *faithful*

Erick [air-ik]: *forever ruler* or *always ruler*

Ethan [ee-thu*h*n]: *strong*

Genesis [jen-*uh*-sis]: *symbol of new beginnings*

Gulliver [gulh-*uh*-ver]: *glutton*

Harry [hair-ee]: *home-ruler*

Holly [hol-ee]: *hollow*

Hunter [hun-ter]: *one who hunts*

Jackson [jack-s*uh*n]: *son of the glorious one*

Jacob [jey-kuhb]: *supplanter* or *take by the heel*

Jason [jey-suhn]: *healer*

Juliet [joo-lee-et]: *symbol of romantic tragedy*

Ricordo [ri-kawr-doh]: *memory*

Kinsey [kin-zee]: *royalty*

Kristen [kris-tuhn]: *follower*

Leah [lee-uh]: *weary*

Lorelei [lawr-uh-lahy]: *alluring enchantress*

Lucas [loo-kuhs]: *bringer of light*

Mallory [mal-uh-ree]: *unfortunate* or *ill-fated*

Owen [oh-uhn]: *noble*

Penelope [puh-nel-uh-pee]: *creator*

Reid [reed]: *woodwind instrument that creates sound*

Richard [rich-urd]: *powerful*

Riley [rahy-lee]: *courageous* or *valiant*

Sarah [sair-uh]: *happy*

Wallace [wol-is]: *stranger*

BEHIND THE
PICKET FENCE

PROLOGUE

My name is Mallory.

Psychologists claim names impact how others perceive us. So wouldn't the way others perceive us impact how we see ourselves? Wouldn't the way we see ourselves impact the choices we make? If names impact a personality, how much of our fate is determined before we know how to talk?

If my name was something simpler like Grace or Jane, would I still be burdened with a tormented soul? Although my old best friend Sarah has a simple name and she was just as burdened as I am. So maybe depth and depression are more about the neurons you were born with and less about what you are named. After all, my sickness is not noticeable at first glance. My neurosis runs deep, and it flows through my blood. The blood that surged through my veins when I was in the womb before my parents named me Mallory.

For most of my life, this sickness inside was the strongest at night. In the morning, I am at peace. I am hopeful. For a few moments, I'm not the stereotypical, self-loathing high schooler in the suburbs who's so bored she decides to be depressed. For a moment, I'm the stereotypical girl in the suburbs with a perfect family, perfect hair, and perfect boyfriend. Recently, mornings have been as bad as the nights. Addicted to my misery, and now it has gained the confidence to lurk in the light. A form of self-inflicted Stockholm Syndrome. I wake up with no hope. Only dread. An inability to get out of bed and live another purposeless day that always ends the same. It will be 9 p.m., and my brain will be sick. And I will look up the cure for my sickness. And I will see there is no cure. And I will think about how I will never recover.

ONE

Mallory [mal-*uh*-ree]:
unfortunate or *ill-fated*

I rummage through the downstairs cabinets for something. Painkillers maybe. I grab a chair and reach for the box on the top shelf. I see a bottle of prescription sleeping pills with my dad's name on it. I hate being someone my parents have to hide medicine from, but here I am taking it, so I can't be too mad at them for treating me like a wounded animal. I walk upstairs in disbelief. In anger. In brokenness. My demons begin to dance all around me. I open my phone to four missed calls from Riley.

They say before you die, your life flashes before your eyes. A movie of all your memories. I stare at the bottle in my hand. The movie begins to play in my mind. A little girl is swimming in the backyard with my dad. She looks pure, innocent even. She looks nothing like me. I look her in the eye. A sadness washes over her face. She knows I'm there. She knows I'm watching. She knows what's coming. She's angry. I have felt her anger inside my body my whole life. She's angry I never let her just be a child swimming without these pills on her mind. She didn't know it was pills. But she knew it was something heavy. Always something heavy. She spent her childhood grieving a childhood I did not let her have. I watch my younger self wait for this moment when the pain will finally stop.

When I was 8, my family went on a week-long volunteer trip to Haiti. I handed out oranges to children living on dirt floors. The kids were happier than I was. I still see their smiles haunting me every night before I fall asleep. I never understood how these children smiled more than I did. They had nothing. But they still smiled. I decided having everything I could ever want inside the picket fence that surrounds our house was the problem. When I got home, I slept in a tent in the backyard for three nights. I ate oranges for breakfast. I sat on the dirt and waited to smile. I never did. Aside from the smelly t-shirt and matted hair, I was still the same sad little girl.

When I was 10, I told mom I had cancer. While she

assured me I was fine, I demanded to see a doctor. A chronic illness seemed to be the only logical reason I felt the way I did, and cancer is the only chronic illness a 10-year-old knows about. The doctor sent me away with a lollipop. The candy didn't make me feel better. Nothing made me feel better. Mom started to call me her little hypochondriac. She didn't understand. I just wanted a diagnosis to explain why I was sadder than those smiling children with nothing. Whether it showed on an X-ray or not, I was sick inside. I have been sick inside for as long as I can remember. I decided in that doctor's office I would be sick inside until the day I died. I began to pray for that day.

When I was 12, I met Sarah. Sarah was also sick inside. She was my very best friend. Sarah talked about wanting to kill herself so much that it was hard to take it seriously. When she cried, it was effortless. No running mascara because she did not wear makeup. She didn't need to. When I was a little girl, I thought makeup was inherently pretty, and that's why people put it on. Then I met Sarah and learned makeup is what makes people pretty. She said she didn't see the point in wearing mascara when it would end up smudged with tears. I explained that's *why* I wore mascara; it's a reason not to cry. Sarah made her sickness sound beautiful. I envied how she made it look beautiful.

My sickness is not romantic. It is not beautiful. It makes me feel ugly. She stopped hanging out with me once she got better. I couldn't blame Sarah for getting better. I waited to get better, but nothing changed. Sarah wears makeup now. I guess she doesn't cry as much anymore.

When I was 14, my school held a mental health assembly. I tried not to laugh when they said suicide was cowardly. Most people don't have the guts to kill themselves. They may say they want to die, but give them the gun, and they will spend the rest of their lives nervously playing with the trigger. It takes guts to pull it. You can call it pathetic, but it certainly isn't cowardly. I tried not to laugh when they said suicide was selfish. If suicide is selfish, that implies one has a choice. Don't those with suicidal ideations have a disease that impairs their ability to reason? How is it selfish when there is seemingly no other option?

When I was 16, my classmate Genesis attempted suicide. The off-putting loner with purple hair who eats lunch alone in a bathroom stall was put on psychiatric hold after taking too many sleeping pills. I remember wondering if it was cowardly of her to swallow the pills or cowardly to call for help afterward. But I don't think she was being selfish. I don't know if Genesis told me what happened for attention or if she just wanted a friend to pity her. Maybe she saw through my disguise and knew I would understand. Regardless, I started stopping by the bathroom to check on her on the way to lunch. Unlike Genesis, depression is not my personality. It is what erased it.

I am 18 now, holding the bottle of pills in my hands.

The movie in my mind is almost over. The credits are about to roll. I am standing with one foot over a cliff. A cliff I've been walking towards my entire life. The view below doesn't look half as appealing as I dreamed it would. But I can't turn around now. I open the bottle of pills as I prepare to make the jump. But there is one more scene I have to endure. I watch myself wake up this morning not knowing the events about to lead me to my fate.

TWO

The sound of my alarm fills me with dread. The thought of going to school, the inevitable argument with my parents about my grades, the idea of my friends talking about college applications—it all makes my soul weary.

I look down and see the results of last night's spiraling. My nails stop halfway up my nail bed. Dried blood on my cuticles. Nasty habit. My fingers look bad again. I'm getting bad again. It's embarrassing not to have control over a behavior my little brother grew out of at seven. I put on Jackson's sweatshirt so I can pull the sleeves over my hands at school. His smell makes my dread subside.

It's early September in the south. The sun pouring into my room makes me feel nauseous. I close the blinds. Every morning, I feel as if I've aged 20 years overnight. I don't remember being 12 or 10 or 8. I have always been and will always be a sad, old soul—a grumpy, old woman who has turned cold to the irredeemable state of this world. I don't want my parents to have to deal with me this morning, and I don't want to deal with them. I text Riley and ask if she can take me to school. I turn on music to drown out the pounding thoughts in my head, wash my face, and apply mascara.

I hear a knock on the bathroom door.

"Come in."

"Please turn that down. It's 7 in the morning. I was out super late. If I can't go back to sleep, you're dead." Camille shuts the door.

My sister makes me smile, even if she is a pain in the morning. I'm glad she's back from college. I don't mean to make her responsible for my mental state, but I worry about it a smidge more when she isn't here. She has been seeing this new guy that she swears she really likes. Of course, she says that about every guy, so I give it two weeks. I love my sister so much it makes me ill with envy. I wish I was her. She goes on drives to listen to sad music when she's "in the mood to cry." I can't relate. I have to purposefully keep sad things out, or I might not get out of bed all day. I wish someone could love me the way I love her. There are limits to how deeply people love me. Boundaries they cannot cross, or they will hurt themselves.

As I put on my leggings, I see my brother Lucas in the doorway. I scream at him and slam the door. I don't like yelling at him, but I was changing, and he knows I need privacy. I am a terrible sister. Who yells that aggressively at their 13-year-old brother over a simple mistake?

It has less to do with someone seeing me change and more to do with the feeling of being watched. Even when I am alone. People are always sitting in the front seat of my mind. Performing for the opinions of those in my head. Exposed at every hour of the day. Emotions I cannot control, anger I wish to hide, words I do not mean.

"...but the door was unlocked," Lucas calls out.

"Will you guys SHUT UP," Camille yells.

I sigh and slide my back against the wall. My hands are cupping my face. My mascara needs to be redone. I do not want to do it.

My parents and Lucas are sitting around the table eating breakfast downstairs. My dad loves to cook, but he doesn't have time to do it as often as he would like. I see my plate on the table. Dad has been making me heart-shaped chocolate chip waffles since I was five. I haven't liked chocolate for years, but I don't have the heart to tell him. Sometimes I suck it up and eat it, but Riley is about to be here. As much as I love my family, I cannot play nice this morning. Not that I want to be mean, but they push my buttons without even trying. They try too hard to love me. As cruel as it sounds, it's annoying.

"Morning, Dad," I say.

"Excited for sushi tonight?" he nudges my shoulder. I nod and force a smile.

I can tell my mom and brother are sad I'm not staying for breakfast. I feel bad, but not bad enough to sit down.

"Mom, are we still going homecoming dress shopping after school?" I ask.

"Yes! I can't wait," she says.

Camille is working at a high-end boutique until she starts her marketing job in the winter. Her degree changed four times while in college. I give it a year before she changes her career path again or finds a man and settles down. Having a family is all she really wants. I'd like to be a mom one day, but I can't imagine making it that far. I don't even know what life looks like an hour from now.

I thank my dad for my packed lunch and see him check his weather app. I know what's coming.

"Mallory, it's 95 degrees outside. I'm sure Jackson won't mind if his girlfriend's not wearing his sweatshirt every day."

Water starts welling in my eyes as I snap back at him. My dad scolds me for having a "disrespectful tone." Everyone, including me, is suddenly yelling. I am reminded why I ask Riley to pick me up most mornings. Lucas tries to defend me, but his butting in makes me angrier.

"Will you all SHUT UP?" Camille yells from the stairwell.

Riley honks her horn. I leave without saying good-bye.

"We're early. Let me say hi to your family," Riley says as I open the car door.

"No, they're being a pain. Let's just go."

"Oh, I'm sorry."

I can feel the judgment in her tone. She thinks I should be more grateful for my family. I *am* grateful. She doesn't have much of a family. She doesn't understand. The depth with which I love them requires a shovel. On days I want to bury myself, I hit them with it in the process.

I don't want to go to English and sit through Sarah raising her hand after every question. Every time I think about Sarah, I cringe. She is the only person who ever fully understood me. I resent her for getting better and leaving me. I used to hate her name. *Sarah*. It sounded sweet, but she was not sweet. She looked big and spoke big, but her name was small, and her name was soft. When Sarah got better, she began to look more like her name— smaller and softer.

I suggest to Riley we skip first-period class and get coffee.

"Can I crash at your place tonight?" she asks. Riley doesn't have a good relationship with her mom and hates staying there. I used to think Riley had the cool mom and I had the strict mom, but the truth was she had a sick mom, and I had a healthy one.

We met in 8th grade when she transferred to my middle school. She sat beside me during morning assembly, and we've been inseparable since. She didn't understand me like Sarah, but she loved me more than Sarah. Sarah was probably not good for me. Riley was good for me. She *is* good for me. She used to spend weeks at a time sleeping at our house. But as she grew older and learned more about her mother's addiction, staying away too long didn't seem responsible. Especially as her mom got worse.

Riley can always sleep over, but tonight Jackson and I have plans to hang out after the party. It has been a while since it's been just us. I try to explain this to her, but I know she gets hurt when I choose Jackson over her.

"It's been a terrible month. I just want to hang out with Jackson alone tonight," I say.

I know how this comes off. She's my best friend, and I should want to be with *her* when I'm sad. But just because I *should* want things doesn't mean my mind agrees. The love I have for Jackson is infatuation. When I am with him, the butterflies in my stomach outdance my demons. It's a blind, drunken love. The love I have for Riley is deeper, but it's a platonic, sober love. A love that screams, *show me your demons, and let's slay them together*. Both are necessary, but I'd rather a drunken love over a sober love today, even if that's not the healthy choice.

I'm harsh with her like I'm harsh with my family. I hate how harsh I am with the people I love. I stare silently out the window waiting for her to say something.

"Why have you had a terrible month?" she asks. All my emotions bubble over and I start to cry. Sometimes I wonder if I'll always live in darkness because I choose to. I know when it gets bad enough, the darkness turns into numbness. I swear the imbalance in my mind is a drug. I let it strangle me until I cannot breathe. The numbness is the only time my thoughts are not racing. But, like drugs, the comedown gets worse every time I indulge my despair.

"I don't want to be here anymore," I whisper.

"I know."

We sip coffee in our booth. I apologize and she places her head on my shoulder. We spend the next hour scrolling and laughing at videos we send to each other. As we leave, I banter with the barista, flirting my way into another coffee. He asks for my number and I politely decline, explaining this extra coffee is for my boyfriend.

"My best friend over there is single, though," I say, nudging him in Riley's direction. He smiles and informs me he has a girlfriend. "Ass-hole," I mutter, take the coffee, and motion to Riley that it's time to leave. I hope she didn't hear.

We get to school and run to the third floor with only a few minutes until the bell rings. With every step, the dread of class increases.

"You head in. I'm going to the bathroom. Tell Mr. Cobalt I'll be in soon."

"Want me to come?" she asks.

I shake my head and smile. I go to the handicapped stall, and sink against the bathroom door. I hate school. The routine, the tests, the bad grades, all of it. The only class I look forward to is volleyball, but even then my favorite hobby has become a chore. It's funny how I would rather mindlessly scroll on my phone on this bathroom floor than put my mind to work. I remember when Camille started high school. She made it sound cool, but I don't feel cool sitting on the bathroom floor.

My fingers feel at home glued to my phone screen. I scroll through other people posting their perfect lives, perfect boyfriends, perfect girlfriends, perfect families, and perfect hobbies. I like how I look through the lens of my meticulously perfected profile. Adults say social media ruined us, but I think it's helped me from going down a dark path. The distraction of comparison.

I habitually check my texts, waiting for one from Jackson. I haven't heard from him all morning. He's probably just stressed about the football game. It's the big rival game; scouts will be there. His dad is the coach. He used to play professionally, so Jackson has a lot to live up to. Riley and I are going to Blaire's party together after the game. I think about which of Camille's outfits I want to wear. I hear a ding on my phone and my heart skips a beat, but it's not Jackson. Riley texted. Mr. Cobalt is asking for my whereabouts. Shoot. Has it really been 20 minutes? I wipe my tears and throw on some powder from my makeup bag. I smile at myself in the mirror. People always tell me I have a pretty smile, but I don't like it. It's fake. An innocent face masking a broken brain. But I know it does wonders—it's why I'm popular and why I get free coffee. My brain is jealous of how put-together my face is. Maybe this is why I punish my skin by picking at my nails. My brain is trying to escape.

I take out the pad of tardy slips from my backpack. I scribble a signature, name, time stamp, and student ID number on the lines. This is one of the few perks of being Genesis' only friend. She is the front desk assistant for one of her electives so she can steal as many empty tardy slips as she wants.

I hand Mr. Cobalt the note. He nods, and I walk to the back of class. The students are talking and comparing answers. I sit at a table with Riley, Jackson, and his teammate Ethan. I nudge Riley before sitting down. She looks stressed.

"Are you okay?" she asks. She's white as a ghost.

"Of course," I say.

It annoys me how often she asks if I'm okay. I know it's out of love, but the line between pity and compassion is thin.

I wrap my arms around Jackson before sitting down.

"Good morning," I say.

He smiles and holds my hand.

"Thanks," he says as I give him his coffee. He looks at me and asks with his eyes if I'm alright. I smile and nod. I hate feeling like a piece of glass people are terrified of dropping. He feels my scabbed fingertips and holds my hands tighter. Usually, he doesn't like holding hands in public. This rare display of affection makes me feel good. He makes me feel like I'm good enough. If I'm good enough for him, I'm good enough for something.

THREE

I remember Jackson kissing me for the first time like it was yesterday. It was first semester of junior year. We were in his car. For our first date, he took me to an Italian restaurant near the school. He was kind and respectful. I still remember what he was wearing—cargo shorts and a striped collar shirt. He looked like he was about to play golf with middle-aged men. It was cute. I remember thinking he was so handsome. Tall, strong, green eyes, and dark brown hair that curled at the ends. I wore a little black dress. I knew I looked pretty. Not because I love gazing in the mirror, but because many guys had told me so. This didn't mean I got all the guys I wanted. I didn't want a relationship, and I didn't do one-night stands, so guys knew not to try. I'm not good at casual and I'm independent, so attaching myself to someone else felt wrong. But I said yes to going out with Jackson because he gave me butterflies—something I hadn't felt since my summer camp crush in 8th grade. I wonder if I will ever be as happy as I was at summer camp. I think that was my peak, raising my hands and crying during the worship songs because everyone else was. Feeling the loud music stir up something inside of me. I thought it was God until I went to a concert and got chills there as well. I figured if it was God at camp, he loved being at trashy concerts, too.

I think being attached makes me feel wrong because I don't know the healthy way to depend on someone. I either have a wall up, or I let someone knock it down and reward them with my heart on a silver platter: a token of my loyalty. Our first date wasn't awkward. We talked for so long. I was surprised he had such deep thoughts while running with such a shallow crowd. Although, I'm sure he thought the same about me.

After the restaurant closed, I suggested we continue talking at Lovers Lot. In hindsight, it was silly of me to say *talk*, because we both knew what people did there. I'd kissed a couple of guys during spin-the-bottle or as a dare, but never like this. Never because I wanted to. To my surprise, we kept talking for a while. He genuinely enjoyed talking to me. I was in the middle of a sentence when he kissed me.

"Sorry, I didn't mean to interrupt. Continue," he said, laughing.

I blushed and couldn't remember what I was rambling on about five seconds earlier.

"It's okay," I said, smiling, pulling him in for another kiss.

I don't remember how we ended up in the backseat. I don't remember him taking off his shirt. I could tell he did this thing often, but I didn't mind. I told myself this was different. He was looking at me differently than the boys would look at me in the closet at a party. His eyes were not dead and blank or looking through me. They were looking *at* me. I had my hands in his hair, and he grabbed them, intertwining his fingers with mine. I started to panic. My gross-looking nails are the ugliest thing about me. It makes me look weird and young and scary and anxious. His fingers opened my hands and started tracing the insides of my palms. That's when he looked down and saw some of the redness I created the night before. He didn't say anything. He just held them up to his lips and kissed them.

He didn't take my shirt off until we started dating. I think having a girlfriend makes him feel like a man. Sometimes, I wonder if he thinks I was made for him. Here to make him feel strong and good about himself. Camille always warned me all teenage boys are disrespectful and only want one thing. She's wrong. Jackson always takes me home at a reasonable time and always thanks my dad for letting him take me out. He even plays video games with Lucas and brings my mom flowers on holidays. My family loves him and so do I. My parents hated Camille's high school boyfriends. I never understood why because they were always nice to me. Camille swears it's because she's the oldest and they are harder on her. They *are* harder on her, not because she is the oldest, but because they expect more from her.

After second period class, Jackson, Ethan, Riley, and I walk to lunch. He holds my hand all the way to the cafeteria. Riley looks angry.

"Are you okay?" I ask.

She nods.

I've sat with Riley, Blaire, and Jamie since freshman

year. Blaire and Jamie are as vapid and vain as they get, but it's hard to find down-to-earth people in high school. Blaire pretends to like me. But that's how girls are. You keep your enemies close. I've tried to explain to Jackson you have to be wary of girls who are always nice. It means something is off. He doesn't understand. It's a different language.

When Jackson and I started dating, he and his two teammates, Caleb and Ethan, started sitting with us. I like Caleb. He is Jackson's best friend. Ethan is stupid, but he is nice enough.

The volleyball player, her best friend, her quarterback boyfriend, two cheerleaders, and two other football players. I don't care about being popular, but I know our table is the one people talk about.

Today, Jackson had to leave lunch early for a student council meeting. His parents forced it on him. He hates it but got voted president without even running.

I see Genesis walk by our table holding a lunch tray. It looks like hotdogs and chili, a notoriously bad meal. I wave at her to come over.

"I'm not hungry," I say and smile. "Have my lunch and throw that garbage away."

She turns red and barely looks at anyone else at the table. I give them a death stare and they all say hi to her. I pull Jackson's chair and motion for her to sit. I know it bothers everyone there, but I don't care. She's wearing fishnets and a red corset top. Her makeup is so dark I can barely see her eyes.

"You and Jackson are totally going to be homecoming king and queen. I voted for you guys just now," she says, stuffing her face with my rice and veggies.

I quickly pull out my phone. I didn't know court nominations had been posted. We all look at the list. I grin seeing our names on the form. Blaire and Jamie, like minions, vote for us. I know Jamie's sad she and Caleb didn't make it.

"This is so good," Genesis says, face full of food.

"My dad makes the best food," I say.

Everyone at the table who has tasted my dad's cooking nods. My phone starts ringing. It's Camille.

"Hey," she says. "Come to the fine arts hall door."

I jump up and run. She surprises me from time to time with food or candy. She really is the best older sister ever. I open the door to see her holding two coffees. I hug her and grab the cup. Even after the one from this morning, I could always use more caffeine.

"You drink coffee now?" I ask.

She laughs. "Take me to the bathroom, will you?"

"Sure, but don't get caught. Take off those sunglasses

so you look like a student. The bathroom by the left staircase is usually empty."

She nods.

I walk back to my lunch table only to find that everyone except Genesis and Riley has left.

"Where is everyone?" I ask.

"They said they had to go to the library to study," Genesis replies.

Riley looks at me and we both roll our eyes. We know damn well they don't study. I smile as Riley tells Genesis she should come to the party Blaire is throwing tonight.

"Yeah, Riley and I will be there. It'll be so fun," I say.

"Will Blaire mind?"

"Of course not. Just say you're with us."

Blaire *will* mind. But she won't tell her to leave if I am the one who invited her.

"Self-harm is attention seeking," my friends muttered the other day when Genesis walked by. As if the attention-seeking part invalidates the self-harm. As if the attention-seeking part isn't another manifestation of the self-harm. To my stuck-up friends' credit, Genesis doesn't cover up her scars. I think she wants people to talk about them. Feeding her misery with the looks people give her.

Self-harm is still self-harm, whether she wants it known or not. Some inflict pain as a cry for help. Some inflict pain as an inward cry. It doesn't quite matter, the reason is still the same: numbing pain by causing more of it. Finding comfort in the fact that there is discomfort you can control. Then comfort yourself for causing it.

I think Genesis was given a bad hand before she had the chance to try. Who names their kid Genesis? Not only is that where Eve ate the damn fruit and doomed us for all eternity, but it doesn't sound pleasant. *Genesis*. What bitter letters, more sour tasting than the apple itself. How can someone named Genesis not have purple hair? This is why I stick to blonde. I could never pull off purple because I could never pull off a name like Genesis. I could never pull off the way she extenuates her stretch marks and scars by wearing fishnets and short shorts. It's captivating. Not in an aesthetically pleasing way, but in a dark way. Of course, most people find it weird and attention-seeking. They aren't necessarily wrong.

FOUR

On my way out of the cafeteria, I pass Coach Cooper, Jackson's dad. We wave at each other. He's nice to me, or at least nicer to me than he is to Jackson. He is proud of his son for getting a girlfriend. I walk to the locker room, stopping at every water fountain I pass to take up time. I used to love volleyball. My parents say I'm not allowed to quit. They worry I'd fail my classes without something requiring passing grades. They are probably right. They also say I'm in a rut and will enjoy it again soon. They are probably right. But I'll never voice that. I do want to love it like I used to. If I just put everything I have into it, I may find enjoyment again. But I'm too tired. Whenever I play, I feel like I'm watching myself from the sidelines.

My teammates are all sportier versions of Blaire and Jamie. Well, except Sarah. Sarah is kind and deep. We smile at each other in the locker room and cheer each other on during practice. It's weird to think about how we used to be so close. I think about her a lot and how she was able to find a reason to live. I don't think she thinks about me much. We met while playing volleyball in 6th grade. It wasn't my fault she stopped hanging out with me. I think I reminded her of a past self she hated so much.

Sarah was so different back then. I don't even recognize her now. In middle school, she told me she wanted to kill herself. And then, one day, she didn't. I catch myself deep in memory staring at her. She smiles and I turn red. I replay Sarah's words from 8th grade when I asked her why she no longer wanted to die.

After changing, we all head to the gym where Coach Jason is waiting. If not for Coach, I'd have pushed harder on my parents to let me take a break from the sport. I've known Coach for a while. He goes to my family's church, but I haven't been in a long time. I think Camille and Coach were friends in high school. Coach Jason has always believed in me. When I look sad, he gives some cheesy advice that doesn't change how I think but makes me feel better. I'd rather talk to him than any therapist or counselor. He calls me into his office while we take a ten-minute break.

"Hey, sport," he says, sliding into his office chair.

His office looks like it was pulled straight out of a fraternity house, except instead of neon beer signs there's a wall covered in inspirational quotes and pictures of his students.

"We need to talk about your attendance. You missed first period class again, and the administration is breathing down my neck about ensuring our athletes are showing up to class. The number of times I have told you this and the number of times you have missed should have already caused me to bench you. I can't have people accusing me of favoritism. This is your last warning. Okay?"

I nod.

I was kind of hoping he was kicking me off, but at the same time, hearing him say he'd given up on me would have crushed me.

"I know you don't want to be here, but you are an asset to this team." He says, giving me a pat on the back.

I try to go above and beyond on the drills for Coach, but my mind is far away. I can't consistently hit a single jump serve. I used to be the best on my team—known for being able to spike any ball. Even if it was a bad set, I could slam it down every time without fail. I was the star player, and now, I spend most games on the bench. Is it wrong that I'm content there? I stay after practice.

"I'm sorry, Coach."

"We all have days."

"It's been weeks since I've made a good play."

"We all have weeks. You still have the game tomorrow. Please take care of yourself. That is the top priority. Do you want to tell me what has been going on?"

I shrug and start crying. "I think God is punishing me," I say.

He shakes his head.

"The people who can be the happiest are also the people who can feel the saddest."

I nodded. He's right. I am happy sometimes, and when I am, I really am. I love people so deeply I have to scream it at them. My happiness will forever have a ribbon of loneliness running through it.

"Do you believe in God?" he asks me.

"I don't know. I mean, I pray sometimes."

Saying 'Dear God' makes my inner monologue seem less lonely. My loneliness has always been confusing for me. I am surrounded by people: my parents, my siblings, my friends, my coach. But I still feel so alone. Maybe I feel alone because I don't know who I am—I feel far away from myself.

"Well, you can't say 'God is punishing me,' if you don't believe in him. Either you are saying that to blame your agony on a fictitious being or you do believe in him. Instead of thinking of your sadness as a punishment, think of it as a blessing. Instead of drowning in it, maybe you just need to learn how to talk to it. The same way you talk to this God you supposedly don't believe in. Hang in there, kiddo."

There's water in my eyes. He has a point. I suppose there must be a God. If there isn't, then who is laughing at us? Who holds our eyes open with strings and lifts us up from bed each morning just to throw us on the ground like puppets? Coach Jason thinks because there's pain, there must be a God. For how would we know pain if there wasn't something greater, something better, something to beat the pain?

I think he's right about my pain proving God is real. But my pain certainly does not prove God is good. If God is real, he is not good. I decide he must be real so I can hold someone accountable for my misery. Does he break us just so he can fix something? Am I so weak I cannot resist his hammer? Have I allowed all of this torment just so that he can feel accomplished?

Seniors get to go off campus for study time, either during the first or last period of the day. I chose the last period, so I don't have to go to 4th period all sweaty. Riley picked that one too, so we could ride home together. She is waiting by her car for me.

"Hey, how was volleyball?"

"Good," I lie.

"Sweet. Well, let me drop you off because I have to finish my college applications. I have two more essay questions to fill out."

"You said the forbidden word, Riley."

We start laughing.

"No, don't do it. I'm sorry," she squeals.

I chase her but she isn't fast enough, and I pinch her.

"When is that word not going to be forbidden?" she pants, getting into the car.

"When I figure out what I want to do with my life."

"Come with me," she pleads.

I groan and turn up the music in the car. We start screaming the trashy lyrics our mothers hate. It isn't good music, but our mothers hate it, so that makes it good. I probably *will* end up following Jackson and Riley to college. They both want to go to Evergreen. The football team for Jackson and the nursing department for Riley. Though I always thought she would pursue art. She gave up on that dream when she learned how few artists really make a career out of their work. Her grandparents are keen on her becoming a doctor. I know I shouldn't follow people to college, but I have no other reason to go. I know no matter what campus I pick, I'll barely show up for class and party too much. At least, that's what Camille made college sound like.

I honestly don't think I'll make it to college. I think I will stay 18 forever. It's not like I'm going to marry Jackson. I know the statistics for high school sweethearts getting married. My mom and dad are the very rare exceptions. But I have no idea where else to go, and Riley and I promised to room together the week we met.

"Thanks for being nice to Genesis today," I say.

"Of course. Did you see what she was wearing?"

We both start snickering. I feel bad for laughing, but even the nicest human would have a hard time holding back. We turn the music up and roll the windows down. I look over and Riley has stopped singing along. Her face looks white again.

"Call me later to pick our outfits for tonight?" I ask.

She nods.

"Riley, are you okay? You've seemed off since science."

She hesitates before speaking. "If I tell you something you are going to hate but I'm only saying because I love you, are you going to be mad at me?"

"Of course not," I assure her.

"Jackson is going to break up with you."

She spits the words out like she has just tasted something rancid. My heart falls out of my chest.

"I'm so sorry." She tries to put her hand on mine and I push it away.

"Don't tell me you're sorry. That would be the best news in the world for you. You would get your two best friends back. No more of us hanging out without you. You get Jackson all to yourself again. This is stupid. Jackson and I are stronger than ever. Riley, he doesn't like you! He never would. You are trying to drive a wedge between us. My gosh, are you ever *not* jealous of me?"

"Me? Jealous of *you*? Look at what you are doing right now. Sabotaging the one good friend you have. What would I be jealous of?"

My rage begins to grow legs and crawl out of my mouth.

"I have plenty of friends. You don't like them because

you don't fit in with them."

"And you do?"

"Yes," I lie. My other friends are plastic. I know she's not in love with Jackson. We are pulling up to my house now.

"Do you know how hard it is to be friends with you, Mallory?"

She is crying. I feel my skin burning.

"When will you see you are not my friend? You are a parasite. I have to be nice to you. Where else would you sleep the next time your mother is too drunk to function?"

"Get out," Riley says.

I've never heard her so serious in my life.

My mom is waiting for me when I get inside.

"Hey, honey, how was your day?"

"Good."

"Are we still going dress shopping? I heard from Camille you might be the homecoming queen. You know Dad and I..."

"Yes, I know Mom. I can't go dress shopping today

anymore."

She was already holding her keys. I know she loves doing mother-daughter stuff, but I can't be the daughter to take dress shopping right now. Some women are not born to be mothers, but my mother was. Some women are not born to be daughters; they are just born.

I start to head for the stairs, but she stops me. She begins to lecture me about my attendance and my grades. I'm ignoring her. I'm too focused on the fact I just called my best friend a parasite. She starts yelling at me for failing some test. I run upstairs and slam my door, smashing my face into my pillow. Through blurred tears, I type in the password to my phone.

Riley, I'm sorry. Send.

I didn't mean it. Send.

Please forgive me. Send.

I'm a terrible friend. I am so mad at myself. I don't realize I'm creating hangnails and peeling them off with my teeth. They start bleeding.

My mom walks in.

"Mom knock!" I yell and throw a pillow in her direction.

She grabs my wrists and drags me to her bathroom

downstairs. She sits me down, runs my hands under water, and applies some cream that stings. Then she paints my tiny nail beds with white nail polish.

"Thank you," I whisper.

She smiles at me, but there are tears in her eyes. "What happened?" she asks me.

I explain to her through deep breaths that I was cruel to Riley and don't think she will forgive me. My mom nods and gives me a big hug. She tells me Riley *will* forgive me. I don't know if she is right this time. I love my mom. I don't tell her that often, but I really do. My phone dings and my heart stops. But it isn't from Riley. It's from Jackson. My heart starts beating again.

Hey, I just left practice. Come over before my game?
I'd love to. Send.

My entire body starts to relax. My reaction to Riley was wrong, but Riley was wrong, too. He isn't going to break up with me. He wants to see me before his game. I bet he's nervous about playing for the scouts. Evergreen has the best team in the state. I'm good at comforting him. I'm good at being a girlfriend. I give good hugs. I give good gifts. I smell good. The problem is, I'm bad at being a person. Those things compete with each other sometimes.

FIVE

I wait on the curb as Jackson pulls up. I kiss him and feel myself calm under his touch.

"How was practice?" I ask.

"Good," he says.

I start rambling about my day and somewhere in there, I mention how Riley said he was going to break up with me. He doesn't say anything, so I fill the silence with laughter. He doesn't think it's funny. I pull my arm from around his and it feels like our skins have severed. He *is* going to break up with me. Part of me is waiting for him to say he loves me and will never leave. But he doesn't. He breaks up with me. I don't even remember the reason he gave, but I don't need one. I should have expected this.

No matter how good I was at being a girlfriend, it didn't matter. I am bad at living.

I accuse him of leaving me for Riley, a narrative I spin so our conversation won't end. I always want to fight it out. Isn't that what love is? If you love someone, you aren't supposed to leave. I know he loves me, so how can he say goodbye? If we fought it out, at least we could have said we tried, but he had made up his mind. I love so hard it looks like violence, and I fight so hard it looks like love. He holds me in the street for a bit.

He asks if we can still be friends. I laugh.

"We never were friends before this. We have never known how to be friends. How can we now, with all our history?" I ask.

He doesn't say anything.

I am simply too hard to love. My tears made his skin so raw his sympathy for me rotted into apathy. Will my hugs always be more suffocating than comforting? Will my "I love yous" always be uttered while my finger is on a trigger? Will my lips forever leave bruises instead of lipstick stains? Had I put him on such a high pedestal he could no longer reach me?

I hear about first heartbreaks all the time. How it's supposed to feel worse than death. When Camille's high school boyfriend broke up with her, she didn't get out of bed for days. But I already can't get out of bed for days, so I don't think tomorrow will look much different. All I can think about is Riley. I grab my phone.

I'm not going to the game or party tonight. Send.

You were right. We broke up. Send.

If Genesis goes to the party, please talk to her. Send.

I wonder how long it will take Blaire to be all over Jackson tonight. I cringe at the thought. Jackson is a good guy, though. He would never do that to me. The problem was not that he was bad but that I was bad. I loathe myself.

Lucas is waiting by the stairs.

"Did Jackson already leave? He didn't say hi."

I don't answer. He follows me to my room and asks if Mom ever left me notes in my lunch in middle school. I nod.

"Did you ever get bullied about them?" he asks.

I shake my head no and give him a hug. He doesn't know how much I need this hug. I tell him I will take care of that kid if he ever makes fun of him again. We laugh.

"We'll have Jackson take care of him," he says, nudging my shoulder.

"Buddy, Jackson isn't going to be coming around anymore."

"Oh."

I start to cry and he put his head on my shoulder.

"Lucas, Mom thinks I'm leaving for the party tonight. Please don't tell her I'm not. I just want to be alone," I say.

He nods.

"Maybe he will come back."

I shake my head.

"He has to come back. He will miss you too much."

He's rambling. I know he means well but it's pushing my buttons. The buttons only family members seem to always get to.

"Just stop! He doesn't love me anymore; you are too young to understand Lucas."

I cry and give him another hug. I don't mean to yell at him.

"Well, I'm old enough to know that I love you," he says.

It was sweet. But it doesn't make me feel better. I ask him to go away. I wipe my tears and go to Camille's room.

She's curling her hair.

"Do I look fat?" she asks.

I shake my head.

"I do. I'm going to change," she says.

"Where are you going?"

"Another date."

My heart sinks. I was hoping she'd be home tonight.

"Will you finally tell me who the lucky guy is when you get back?" I ask.

She laughs and nods.

I leave the room and let out the tears I've been holding back. I could've told Camille what happened. She'd have canceled and stayed here with me all night, but I don't want to ruin her date. I lie back on my bed, and it feels like something is crushing me. As if every time Jackson and I kissed, our love grew heavier. I didn't know it at the time because the butterflies made me feel light. But now, the heaviness is suffocating me. I wish I didn't kiss him when I got into his car. No, I wish I kissed him longer. I wish I was dead. I remember what Sarah said in 8th grade when I asked her why she didn't want to die anymore.

I take a deep breath. I don't only wish I was dead because my boyfriend broke up with me. But I do wish I was dead. The only difference is now I can't distract myself with his touch or voice. I curl myself in a ball for a long time. Just thinking and not thinking. Lucas comes in wearing some country western outfit.

"Looking good, Lucas," I say.

I'm trying so hard to be kind. He smiles and runs out.

Mom knocks on the door a few minutes later.

"Hi, sweetie. I just wanted to say bye," she calls out.

"Bye," I say.

She knocks again.

"I'm changing," I lie.

She opens the door. "Sorry, I couldn't hear you..." She sees me crying. "...baby, I'm so sorry. I love you."

I didn't even have to tell her. Mothers just know.

"Do you want me to stay home tonight?"

"No."

That damn phrase. *I love you*. Of course, she does. Because she has to. Just like Riley has to, or she will feel responsible for whatever I do to myself. Of course, Camille and Lucas love me because they have to. Of course, Blaire and Jamie love me because they think I make them popular. No one chooses to love me. I start to feel the burning sensation in my skin again.

"Why?" I ask my mom.

She looks confused.

"Why do you love me?" I clarify.

"Because you are my daughter," she says.

My heart sinks. She loves me because she is required to. She loves me because not loving me would make her a bad mother. Is love ever unconditional? If God is out there like Coach Jason insists, he certainly doesn't love me without condition. He loves me because if he didn't, it would make him a failure.

For who hates their own creation? I wonder if that God up there *likes* me. I think I would rather be liked than loved. At least if I am liked, someone chooses to like me. If God exists, he does not like me. If God exists, I certainly do not like him.

"But you don't like me," I say.

"I do like you. I *love* you."

I don't know why *she* is the one crying.

"You resent me. I make you a bad mom because moms aren't supposed to have a hard time loving their kids. You don't know how to love me. You don't know how to help me."

I'm crying. I don't mean what I'm saying.

"You are right about one thing, I don't know how to help you," she scolds.

"Well, start by leaving me alone."

I get up and slam the door. I start crying harder. I wait for her to open it and hug me, but she doesn't. I am alone and I am a cruel daughter. I was not born to be a daughter.

I was just born. I return to my ball of shame.

My dad comes into my room and doesn't say anything. My mom must have told him. He sits down and rubs my shoulder. I curl up on his lap, and he smooths my hair. I've not been this close to my dad in years. I start crying.

"Looks like sushi will be just us tonight, sport. Come on, you need to get out of the house."

"I can't go to sushi, Dad. Can I just stay here?"

He smiles and nods. "Whatever you need. Do you want ice cream?"

I shake my head. "I think I just want to be alone."

He nods. "I'm not going to give you the big break-up talk where I tell you teenage boys don't know how to love yet and one day you will find a guy who does. I know you don't want to hear that, so I will just say I love you, Mallory. Please talk to me when you are ready to hear it."

I stop him before he leaves, "I love you, Dad."

"Me too... more than you know," he says.

My dad loves me because he has to *and* because he wants to. Sometimes, I think no one understands me like he does. He understands me because he's what I could be if I ever learned to diffuse the pressure inside. He is a healthy version of me. This also means he is nothing like me, because who am I without my hurt? I've become so comfortable with my tears that I'd surely die of thirst without them.

After mindlessly scrolling on my phone for an hour or two, I decide to go to the party tonight. It will be a good distraction. Part of me wants to be in the same room as Jackson for revenge and the other part of me wants the peace of being near him. I wonder how he is doing at the game. I hope he doesn't do well and needs me to comfort him.

SIX

I'm waiting in Camille's room when she gets home from her date. She comes in all smiley and blushing. I roll my eyes at her and she laughs.

"Camille. Jackson broke up with me."

She drops her bag.

"What happened?"

I tell her everything, from my fight with Riley to the car ride with Jackson. She always gives the best advice. I try to truly listen as she starts talking.

"First breakups feel like the world is ending and everyone around you is moving along in fast motion because you haven't learned that you can, and will, fall in love again. If there are such things as soulmates, they aren't found. They are made. Just because a good relationship ends doesn't mean it was bad. It just means it was completed. You are one person closer to the one you will marry."

"You know this heartbreak feeling? I feel this all the time. My heart is always aching, always breaking," I tell her.

"I know," she says. I lay my head on her shoulder.

"My friends are all going to Blaire's house after the game."

"Well, you're going to go, aren't you? You can't let a boy ruin a good night. It's Friday. Come on."

I smile.

"You can wear one of my outfits and I'll do your makeup."

I pick out an outfit that she never lets me wear. A black lace top and jeans. She does my makeup all fancy. I think it is too much, but she insists I look perfect. I ask her about the mystery man while she does my hair. She laughs and tells me she wanted to keep it a secret until it was official. I look at her confused. I have no idea who she could be talking about. I forget about Jackson and Riley for a moment.

"Coach Jason and I are dating!" she says excitedly.

My immediate reaction is to start laughing. But then I realize what she just said. I shake her off from doing my hair and stare at her.

"Volleyball is the ONE thing that is MINE, and you've taken it. Where the hell do you get off Camille? Let me have ONE THING."

Camille seems genuinely surprised by my reaction, which I find comical. How can she actually think I'd be okay with this? He never wanted me to stay on the team. He was just cozying up next to my sister behind closed doors.

"And what is going to happen when you break up with him? At what point does this end up being one of your dozen two-week relationships? What then, huh? What happens when you get bored? Out of everyone in this damn city, you pick one of the only consistent people in my life. You never think of anyone but yourself. What happens when this ends? What does that mean for me?"

She looks at me with a straight face. Her eyes start welling. She purses her lips together and starts shaking her head like my mother. I grow angrier.

"Say something!" I yell.

She walks towards me with her arms out as if to hug me.

"You are just hurting and taking it out on me."

51

"Don't touch me." I push her away. "My entire life, I've lived in your shadow. Everything you did was better. Sports is the one thing I have. You couldn't live with that, could you?"

"Just because you are so miserable doesn't mean I have to be! You know you *can* be happy for people. You are the only one who has ever compared yourself to me. That sucks, but it doesn't mean I should feel bad about being happy. You don't have to be a bitch. You know Mallory, other people have problems too. You wouldn't know about any of them because you don't ask. You use me as a sponge to soak up all your tears and give me NOTHING in return. Maybe this is why Jackson and Riley are done with you. Take off my clothes and leave."

I am fuming. I throw her clothes on the ground and storm out. I know sisters say things all the time they don't mean. She doesn't ever let what I say get to her. To be a sister is to see the ugliest sides and love them anyway. That was not why I was mad. I was mad because, this time, she was right. I did not realize volleyball was the only good thing I had until she took it away. I suppose my sadness is the only thing that is truly mine.

I just want to be a child on my dad's lap again. I pick out an outfit from my closet and put it on. I'm determined to have a good night tonight. These are the times

I'm glad Blaire and Jamie are my friends. They will tell me I look hot, give me a shot, and gossip about everyone else in the room. Normally, I would find this boring, but today I feel empty. I have to fill myself with something, even if it is shallow and stupid and drenched in liquor and everything I hate. I guess it's better to be hungover than dead.

Riley still hasn't answered my texts. I need to talk to her, although I doubt she'd go to that party without me. She doesn't drink with her mom being an alcoholic, and she doesn't like the girls in our group. I selfishly hope Genesis won't be there. I just want to be vain and popular and normal and pretty and single and too stupid to be sad for one night. If ignorance is bliss, I want to drink and dance until I am too numb to feel anything. I walk downstairs, and my dad is sitting alone watching TV on the couch.

"Hey, sport, is everything okay? I heard yelling."

"Did you know Camille is dating Coach Jason? I can't believe she would do that to me."

"I heard something about it, yes. He is a great guy. I think it could be good."

I shake my head and roll my eyes. "Well, how about you come watch this show with me? Remember when you were little and we watched this together every Friday? I'm going to make a sandwich. Do you want one?"

53

I loved Friday nights with my dad, but I'm not ten anymore. Friday nights aren't supposed to be spent with my dad.

"No, I am okay. I made plans."

"You are always making plans. I thought you didn't want to leave the house tonight," he laughs.

I do not find it funny.

"I don't think I should be alone right now."

I realize how that must have come across since he would be with me if I stayed. I wish I could sit in silence with him, but I can't. I have to be busy. Be out. The comfort would give me discomfort. In a crowd of people who don't care about me, I don't have the time to question my sanity. But my father would ask about how I was doing in a safe space where I'd have to come to terms with reality. I get a notification on my phone that my ride is here, and I say bye to my dad. I'm filled with guilt, but not enough to make me stay.

We haven't even left the block when I get a text. It's not from Riley. It's not from Jackson. It's from Genesis. I'd forgotten she even had my phone number.

Hey Mallory. I just wanted to tell you that I walked in on Riley and Jackson kissing. I'm sorry. I don't know if you are still coming, but I'm leaving the party. It blows. No one is talking to me.

I tell the driver I've given him the wrong address and ask him to drop me off here. He's confused, but I have no desire to explain. I just hand him a ten and shut the door. I'm right next to the neighborhood park. I walk over and sit on the slide.

I look at my phone and re-read her text before throwing up. I feel like I might pass out. I can see my house from this high up on the slide. I look up at the sky and take several deep breaths. I decide to wait for my mom and Lucas to get home and go to bed before I walk back. As much as I hope Lucas had fun, I don't want to hear about it. My phone starts ringing like crazy and over the next 30 minutes, Riley calls me eight times.

I was wrong about Riley. I thought she loved me because she felt a duty or obligation to be loyal to me. But if this was true, she wouldn't have kissed Jackson. Maybe she is like God. Loving me to fix something or to feel accomplished. They both failed. I am choosing between smashing my phone against the ground or scrolling on it. I wish I could say I had control over my emotions, which is why I didn't throw my phone, but truthfully, I didn't have the willpower to break my one distraction.

I see Camille get in her car while talking on the phone. The thought of her going somewhere with Coach Jason made me angrier. The picture in my mind of them together is replaced by Riley and Jackson kissing. Why couldn't it have been Blaire? I thought I was crazy for accusing them. I felt like a bad human, but I was right. Maybe I should listen to my gut more often. Right now, my gut is begging me to die.

Most people's hurt is about something tangible. They can name it. I've never been able to pinpoint the cause of this pressure I carry on the inside. Now I have Jackson, Riley, Camille, and Coach to pin it on, but I can't. The only thing I am able to blame is oranges. The fruit I gave those starving children in Haiti when I was eight years old. I remember how they smiled. No matter what or who I try to point at, this pressure is chronic. It does not depend on circumstances to better or worsen, only to distract. But there is nothing and no one to distract me anymore.

SEVEN

The pill bottle feels at home in my hand. The movie in my mind is over. The credits are rolling. There is a fire brewing in my body. My skin is burning. The pills are begging me to consume them. How can I refuse? My thoughts are too loud. I can't think. How can I ignore the volume button? I can turn the noise down. I can turn the noise off.

I think about Sarah from the volleyball team. I think about Sarah from middle school. She used to cut people with her words. I hated her for telling me she wanted to kill herself because it would mean depression really could win. The thought of wanting to die seemed far away in my head, like a floating object that did not belong to me. But when Sarah would speak it aloud, that thought got closer. It would cling to me. So close it touched my skin. Now it's a part of me. There is no separating me from my fate. Eventually, Sarah stopped saying she wanted to die. She quit nicotine and broke up with her toxic boyfriend. She convinced her battered mother to leave her abusive father. She even went to church. She was starting over. She stopped hanging out with me. I may have been part of the problem. After all, two depressed people rarely pull each other out of the hole, but rather accidentally dig a deeper one together.

I started to resent her. I did not drown myself in alcohol or nicotine, I did not have a toxic boyfriend, I lived with both of my parents, and I went to church. But none of that made me better. I didn't realize at the time those things were not the cure for Sarah. It was just a side effect of the cure. But what was the damn cure? At the end of 8th grade, I asked her why she didn't want to die anymore. Sarah's words earned a permanent spot in my mind:

> *"Whenever I thought I wanted to die, I started thinking about the people who loved me. I relive the last moments I had with them. Going through their days in my mind…"*

The school bell cut her off. I never got to hear the last part. But even then, I thought this was a lousy answer. In fact, it wasn't an answer at all. She should know that thinking about our loved ones doesn't make people like us decide we don't want to die. It makes us feel guilty about wanting to die. And our shame gives us another reason to feel we shouldn't be here. I hated her answer more than I hated when she spoke about killing herself. We never talked about it again.

Every word we now speak to each other in the locker room, words about stupid rumors or clothes or Coach, leaves a lingering heaviness between our breaths. As if her eyes are holding on to guilt and expressing a desire to help, while my eyes are seeking an apology and screaming for help. But we don't acknowledge it. Sarah looks more like her name now—smaller and softer. I don't know how to speak to this version of her. I know being healthy does not mean she judges me, but her softness makes me realize how hard I am. How unhealthy I am.

The pills are in my hands now. The burning is hot. The noise is loud. My feet are dangling off the cliff. I bring my hand to my mouth. I remember what Sarah said. I think about the people I love. I think about their days in my mind.

EIGHT

Harry [hair-ee]:
home-ruler

    Harry admires how beautiful Juliet looks asleep next to him. Just the shape of his wife's face asleep on the pillow reminds him of the morning after their wedding. Harry looks at his work clothes laid out—another day of pretending to care about a company that doesn't care about him. He hates being a tiny part in a big machine. He's doing what he swore in his 20s he would never do. Harry is not excited about work; he is rarely excited about work, but today, he especially lacks enthusiasm.

    Harry always thought Richard respected him. He used to be the first pick for projects or crisis management, but Richard has been acting cold recently. *It must be his old age. Although this attitude shift seems to be directed solely towards me.*

Harry hates that no matter how much he tries, he too, grows more irritable each birthday. With Richard retiring any year now, it's between him and his coworker Jacob for the new CFO position. Harry and Jacob have an unspoken agreement—Harry does not like Jacob, and Jacob does not like Harry.

After remembering it's Friday, Harry gets out of bed. Ever since Camille started pre-k, Friday has been waffle day. Mallory likes hers with chocolate chips, Lucas likes his with bananas, and Camille likes to sleep in. *Some things never change.*

He walks to the bathroom to brush his teeth and stares at a man he doesn't recognize in the mirror. A middle-aged man with a few gray hairs and newly formed wrinkles. He wonders where his fourties went. In his head, his children are still babies who run to the door when he gets home from work. He's getting old, tired, grumpy, and cynical, and he hates it.

"The fan is still making that ticking sound. I got no sleep," Juliet says as she wakes up.

Harry sighs and heads to the kitchen. He used to look forward to Friday mornings—silence and solitude before the kids wake up. It used to be his only time of peace and quiet, but he now finds himself missing the noise in the house. Lucas just turned 13 and spends most of his time playing video games or reading comic books. Mallory is in the "too cool for my family" stage, so she'd rather spend time with her friends. Camille is 22. She enjoys being with her family, but before he knows it, she will have a family of her own.

Harry feels at peace in the kitchen, even if it's just pouring batter into the waffle maker. He used to dream of owning his own restaurant, but at the ripe old age of 49, he knows that dreams are simply an escape from the life you are supposed to live.

"Good morning, honey," Juliet says, tying the belt of her robe. He smiles and hands her a mug. "You look stressed," she says as she turns on the coffee maker. He shakes his head.

Harry and Juliet also have an unspoken agreement: they lie to each other. They don't press, so they don't argue. Harry finds it's best for their marriage when he keeps things to himself. For her sake, of course. There are unspoken lines they don't cross. Harry would never cheat on her and she wouldn't cheat on him. But when he kisses her, it feels like he is cheating on the woman he married. He's sure she feels the same.

Truthfully, Harry is extremely stressed. He was supposed to pitch the new model today, but Jacob pitched it to Richard behind his back and took all the credit.

Juliet sets the table. Five plates. She walks over to the family calendar taped to the refrigerator.

"I am taking Lucas to the band banquet tonight," she yawns.

"That'll be fun. I will be gone for dinner anyway. I am taking Mallory and Camille to that sushi place they like. Planned it a while ago. You know how you have to book in advance with those two." Harry laughs.

He looks at the set table and reminds himself this is why he puts up with the corporate lifestyle. For moments like this. The sound of his kids getting ready upstairs, his mother's silverware on the table, and his high school sweetheart cutting strawberries beside him feels exactly the way he imagined it as a boy. Before the world got ahead of him. Before the kids outgrew them. Before they outgrew each other. Juliet scribbles *sushi* on the calendar for today next to Harry and the girls' names. *Probably so the girls don't forget again.*

Lucas walks sluggishly into the kitchen wearing a vintage band t-shirt. He never fit in with the boys in elementary school, no matter how many of his sports teams Harry would coach. This year, he's found a new group of friends—wannabe outsiders he tries to impress. *His name-brand pants and suburban kid haircut aren't doing him any favors.*

"Good morning," Lucas mumbles, slumping into a chair. Harry doesn't mean to tune out Lucas going on and on about his science test. He nods at Lucas's remarks as he sips his coffee. Work is forgotten for a moment. Mallory rushes downstairs.

"Morning," she says, throwing her backpack over her shoulder.

"Good morning, Mallory. How'd you sleep?"

"I didn't."

"Why not? You need to sleep, Mallory."

"I know, Dad. I was doing homework," she scoffs.

Juliet's eyes shoot Mallory a warning.

"Well, I made your favorite," he says.

"I've got to run. Sorry."

"You need to eat something."

"Not hungry."

"How about one for the road? I put in extra chocolate chips."

"I said I'm not hungry."

She's wearing sweatpants and her boyfriend's sweatshirt. It's 95 degrees outside.

"You're not going to be hot in that sweatshirt? I don't

think Jackson will mind if you don't wear it for one day," Harry says with a smile.

Mallory turns red. "Why do you always care about what I'm wearing? You don't tell Lucas his outfits look weird. You're always criticizing me."

Harry sighs. He was just trying to help. She looks like she wants to cry but yells instead. Harry yells at her for yelling. She flinches. Juliet yells at Harry for yelling at Mallory for yelling. Camille yells at them for yelling while she's trying to sleep. Lucas starts laughing. This is not an uncommon morning in the Bakersfield household. A few seconds of silence go by before Lucas tries to talk his way out of tonight's banquet.

Harry takes a deep breath. "Mallory, do you want a ride to school? It's on the way to work."

"What? Uh, no. Riley's almost here," she says without looking up from her phone.

Juliet clears her throat. "Does she want to come grab a bite?" she asks.

Mallory doesn't hear her. A car honks outside.

"Bye, sweetheart," Harry calls after her.

"Dad, you should take me to school," Lucas says.

"Of course, bud."

Harry throws out Mallory's stack of waffles and grabs his keys.

Harry had assumed when Mallory got her first boy-friend, he wouldn't be as hesitant since he'd already gone through it with Camille, but he's still as protective as ever. After all, he was a teenage boy once.

She's too young to have her heart broken by a guy who doesn't know what it means to love.

But he would never say that to her. He can't, or the invisible wedge between them would grow. He knows she doesn't mean to run so far away. But the faster she runs, the older she grows. And the more she grows, the more he misses. And the more he misses, the more he doesn't recognize. And the more he doesn't recognize, the more he wants to understand. And the more he tries to understand, the more she yells at him for pressing. And the more she yells at him for pressing, the more he yells at her for yelling. The more they yell, the less they talk.

"Don't you ever get too cool for waffle day Lucas."

"Never," he says, as they pull up to the school.

Harry laughs. *At least one of my kids thinks I'm cool.*

As Harry drives to work he can't get the image of Mallory flinching out of his mind. For a split second, there was fear in her eyes.

Who does she think she is? Acting like a wounded puppy after treating her entire family like garbage? I yelled at her when she was little and didn't clean her room. Not in a scary way, but in a "respect me and take me seriously so I don't have to raise my voice again because I don't want to" kind of way. She never flinched then. She knew Daddy would never hurt her. Did she forget it's my job to protect her? Did she forget we are on the same team?

NINE

Harry is the treasurer of an oil and gas company. He sits at his desk and works on spreadsheet after spreadsheet before going to the break room to pour himself another stale, but necessary, cup of coffee. Jacob is talking to one of the other finance guys in the hall. Harry hears his name.

"Well, you don't need to worry about Harry. We should be looking for a new treasurer soon."

Harry's blood boils as Jacob takes his seat next to him.

He sees a new photo of Jacob's daughter, Sarah, on his desk. Mallory and Sarah used to hang out when they were younger. Harry scoffs, knowing Sarah certainly has no pictures of her father around. Jacob's never been to a single one of Sarah and Mallory's volleyball games.

"I heard you presented the cash flow model to Richard yesterday," Harry says.

Jacob nods without looking up.

"...without any of my analysis," Harry says, growing more frustrated.

"The model was just fine. I don't need your analysis."

"It could have been more extensive."

"Mind your own damn business Bakersfield."

"You keep your hands out of my models," he says, interrupted by Richard motioning for Jacob to join him in his office.

Harry knows everyone despises Jacob and his big mouth as much as he does, but Richard seems to appreciate Jacob's ambition and workaholism.

He takes out the stale bread and turkey he begrudgingly packs himself every morning. It tastes even more bland than usual. He takes another bite before putting the sandwich back in the bag.

He spends the next hour plugging figures into spreadsheets, but numbers do a terrible job of distracting him from wondering what Jacob and Richard might be talking about. He watches through the glass doors as Richard shakes Jacob's hand.

Harry opens the analysis he was supposed to pitch today. He decided he'd show Richard anyway.

See how Jacob likes it when people go behind his back for once.

Harry's phone rings. He takes a deep breath before answering.

"Hey, Camille, now's not a great time," he says.

"I was going to ask if I could grab dinner with you another night. Jason wants to take me out and I think he's going to ask to make it official."

"That's awesome. I really like Jason. Have fun tonight. I have to run." He hangs up as Jacob walks out of Richard's office.

"Pack your things. You're done," Jacob says.

"Who do you think you are, telling me..."

"I am the new CFO. I expect your resignation by 2:00."

Harry packs his things and leaves without another word. Other than the disappointment this will cause his wife, this might be the best thing that's ever happened to him. But the only thing worse than being a slave to the corporate world is unemployment.

It's 1:00. Harry sits in his car and turns up the music. He tries to convince himself God has a plan. *Easy words to say to your wife and children who are not worried about supporting a family.*

He drives to the local bar and grill by his house, orders a beer, and watches the game. This place used to be booming when he first got married, before bad food and worse management ran it under.

"Rough day?" the bartender asks, handing him another beer.

Harry laughs. "You could say that."

"Tell me about it, boss just told us this place is going on the market. The wife's gonna kill me when she finds out I have to look for another job. It's brutal out there."

"Cheers to that," Harry says, raising his glass. The bartender pours himself a drink and looks down.

"Oh c'mon? Have a drink. Not like they can fire you."

The bartender laughs. "Cheers."

"What's a place like this sell for anyway?" Harry asks.

Harry imagines what Juliet would say if he told her

he'd bought a restaurant. She would think he's crazy.

"You interested or something?" the bartender laughs.

"No, just curious," Harry says. *Dreams are dreams for a reason. An escape from the life you are supposed to live.*

He sits there all afternoon. He contemplates picking up his phone and telling Juliet he has to look for another job. She will predictably go into a frenzy and offer solutions he didn't ask for.

After a couple more beers, Harry leaves the bar to get home at the usual time. Juliet is sitting at the table when he walks in the door. He gives her a hug.

"Long day today?" she asks him. Harry nods. "Anything specific?" Harry shakes his head no.

"I had a long day too. Lucas made me get him early from school again."

"Well, don't keep picking him up, or he will keep asking you to," Harry interjects.

She sighs. "I was just expressing why I was tired." She looks at him. "Have you been drinking?"

"Barely."

She scrunches her eyebrows at him like his mother used to do when he was in trouble.

"I can't deal with the nagging right now."

Juliet walks over to the bedroom and starts getting ready for the banquet. Harry places his face in his hands.

This is how their arguments usually go. She talks so she can feel understood. He forgets this and tries to fix whatever she is upset about. He can never do enough and she never feels heard.

Camille walks through the door beaming.

"How was work?" she asks.

"Fine," Harry lies. "Nervous for tonight?"

Camille squeals and runs upstairs as Lucas drags his feet to the kitchen, wearing a western outfit and an annoyed expression.

"Looking sharp," Harry says, trying not to laugh.

"Lucas, let me say bye to your sisters, then we can head out," Juliet says coming in to grab her wallet.

"How was school today, Lucas?" Harry asks.

Juliet darts her eyes at Harry, shaking her head. He drops it and asks Lucas about the new drum solo he's been practicing. Mallory and Juliet are yelling upstairs. Juliet comes back with tears in her eyes.

"Jackson broke up with Mallory," she says.

Harry breathes a sigh of relief followed by sadness knowing this will crush her.

"Go talk to her, Harry."

He nods. "You guys have fun."

"I'll try," Lucas says.

Harry walks upstairs and sees Mallory curled up in a

73

ball on her bed. He sits next to her without saying anything. He rubs his hands on her shoulders and she curls beside him. It feels like she's his little girl again. There are so many words he wishes he could say, but he thinks she just wants him to hold her.

"Looks like sushi will just be me and you tonight, sport. Come on, you need to get out of the house."

"I can't go to sushi, Dad. Can I just stay here?" she asks.

He smiles and nods. He asks her if she wants ice cream but she just wants to be alone.

"I love you, Dad," Mallory says as he walks away.

"I love you, too...more than you know."

Harry sees himself in Mallory more than any of his other kids. He understands her sadness because she gets it from him. He knows she will get better. He knows her life will be a long road of getting better, and then worse, and then better again. He knows it's going to be why Mallory is able to love deeper than most. She loves like he loves. She hurts like he hurts.

Harry goes downstairs, grabs another beer, and turns on the TV. The house is empty, aside from Mallory upstairs. He grabs his sleeping pills, hoping to sleep away the mess of today.

The sound of Camille's car pulling into the driveway wakes him up.

She walks in smiling.

"How was it?" he asks.

"We're dating!"

"Attagirl," he says. "You should tell Mallory!"

He turns up the TV and tries not to think about work. He was hoping to sleep through Juliet and Lucas coming home to delay breaking the news as long as possible. He hears the girls yelling upstairs and gives up sleeping.

After a couple of episodes, Mallory comes downstairs in a shirt that would have been considered undergarments when Harry was in high school. He bites his tongue. *Not the time.*

"I heard yelling, is everything okay?" he asks. She is not happy about Camille and Jason. *Another conversation for a different time.*

"Sit and watch TV with me?"

"I'm sorry, Dad, I already made plans."

"I thought you didn't want to leave the house

tonight," he laughs.

She doesn't smile. She looks like she might cry.

"I don't think I should be alone," she says. He nods.

"Have fun. Maybe we can get sushi for lunch tomorrow. You owe me one."

"Yeah, maybe," she says and walks out the door.

"I love you," he calls out.

He walks to the kitchen and gets out the bread and peanut butter. The house is quiet again. He gets angry thinking about Jacob sitting at Richards's desk tomorrow, he imagines sitting there instead, but that doesn't feel right either. He takes a bite of the sandwich and stares out the window, vowing to never to eat another stale sandwich again. He takes out the ground beef, vegetables, spices, and butter, to make himself a proper dinner. Not so much because he thinks he deserves a good meal, but because cooking is the only thing that might distract his mind.

"Smells really good, Dad," Camille says, grabbing her keys.

"Do you want some?" he asks.

"I wish, but I have to run. Riley's in some kind of trouble."

She looks at the plate in front of him. "Well, maybe one bite." She stuffs a forkful in her mouth.

"Oh my gosh. I told you, you should've been a chef." Harry smiles as she grabs her keys and runs out the door.

Camille's words ring in his mind as he remembers his younger self. What would he have done? Harry paces for a bit before picking up the phone. He calls the bar and grill and makes an offer. It feels right. It feels crazy. It feels good.

In bed that night, Harry admires how beautiful Juliet looks next to him. Just the shape of his wife's face falling asleep on the pillow.

"You are the most beautiful woman I've ever seen," he says.

She smiles and gives him a kiss.

"Is Richard still being cold to you?"

"Yes. But I have it figured out," he says.

"You always do."

Harry falls asleep without taking his sleeping medication for the first time in a long time.

TEN

Riley [rahy-lee]:
strength

Riley eyes the envelope on her side table before heading to the kitchen. She almost opens it. Her mom, Bella, is passed out on the couch with an open bottle of vodka in front of her. She switches it out for a cup of water, pouring the liquor down the sink. In hindsight, it's probably counterproductive because her mom will just waste money on another bottle today. She checks the calendar on the fridge.

"Mom. Mom. Mom."

It's like nudging a statue.

"Mom!" she yells.

"What? Gosh, why are you screaming?"

"You have a morning shift today." Riley throws her the stained apron.

"I knew that. I had an alarm set," Bella says. Riley taps the phone next to her. It's dead. "I could've sworn I plugged that in."

"Right."

Riley thinks she still looks a little drunk.

"Don't give me that judgmental tone," Bella says, popping a Xanax.

When Riley was in middle school, her mom took her to the doctor and convinced them she had crippling anxiety. Riley was prescribed a small dose of Prozac and then Zoloft. Insisting it kept getting worse, Bella eventually found a doctor willing to prescribe Xanax. She told Riley she had bad anxiety and couldn't afford medication. She explained the prescription had to be in Riley's name since her grandparents paid for her insurance. It made sense to Riley when she was younger.

"Have a good day, sweetie. I love you," Bella calls out.

Riley grabs her backpack and heads for the door.

Bella's biggest regret is not being a present mom. So she acts like she has it all together, as if Riley doesn't wake her up for work most mornings. As a little girl, Riley always envied that when she stayed at Jackson's house his mom would wake *them* up for school.

Riley was the product of a one-night stand. Her parents met at a bar. She was born in a bed of lies. Bella was only 19 years old. Her father was 35. They both lied to each other about their real age. He didn't tell her that he was on a business trip with a wife across the country. And she lied to him about being on birth control. He had a family with children 8 years younger than her. She gave him her number the next morning, but he never called. Riley learned at a young age Bella is starved for love. She lives to find it but never does.

Riley learned at a young age that just because you are beautiful on the outside doesn't mean anyone wants to know what's on the inside. Riley learned at a young age that her mom is easy because she wants to be loved, but no one seems to love her because she is easy.

Riley doesn't look anything like her mom. Bella has deep almond-shaped eyes and a petite face. She is skinny and short with long silky black hair and big lips. Riley is the polar opposite. Average height, average build, big nose, and thin lips. Her mom is Japanese and her father is caucasian. In sixth grade, some boy told her she had the ugly qualities of both races. She called her mom from the school nurse's office and told her she wanted to go home. Bella ended up causing a scene by talking to the boy after school. It made things worse. Riley sat in the car and cried. Instead of being the ugly kid, she was now the ugly kid with the hot mom who dressed like a teenager. This was somehow worse.

It wasn't until they almost got evicted that Bella finally tracked down Riley's father on social media and demanded child support in exchange for her silence. Riley grew up thinking her dad was some deadbeat who left once he learned she was pregnant. It wasn't until she was 15 that her mom admitted the truth—her father never knew she existed. Riley didn't have much of a reaction. She didn't know what the right reaction would be. She was 15 when she saw the first picture of her father. She looked like him. She didn't want to see pictures of her adult half-siblings. She didn't want to know what she missed out on—the opportunities all the lies stole from her.

Her father immediately flew down and demanded a DNA test. When it came back positive, he started giving Bella handouts. He was nice enough when Riley met him. He looked a lot different than she imagined her dad looked like growing up—older, put together, and serious. He gave her an awkward hug and didn't say much. He saw one of her art pieces and told her she was talented. She holds on to that every day. Her dad may not know her, but he thinks she is good at something.

He bought Riley a car last year. She thinks doing that made him feel less bad about her living alone with Bella. Riley was able to quit working at the boutique down the street once he started sending money every month for clothes and such. He says she can pick any university to attend. Sometimes she feels bad for taking a stranger's money, but her mom says he's some big-shot lawyer in New York. So, the amount he gives is spare change for him.

Bella's parents are immigrants from Japan. They both worked 60-hour weeks to give her a good life. They had high hopes and even higher expectations. Bella was not gifted at school. She ran with the wrong crowd. She barely graduated high school. While her parents dreamed of a doctor-daughter who went to one of the big universities, she settled for the only school she could get into. She dropped out freshman year and started working full-time. When her parents found out she was pregnant, they were livid. They told her she could only continue living with them if she went back to school. She started sleeping at her friend's house the next day.

When Riley was in elementary school, her mom started dating an older man from Oklahoma that she met online. She moved in with him after three months. Riley didn't want to leave her friends, so she moved in with her grandparents for about a year until her mom's relationship ended. When Bella moved back, she rented an apartment and started working at the diner. Riley had the choice to continue living with her grandparents or move back in with her mom. She chose her mom. She preferred making her own rules. Bella lets her do what she wants.

Riley loves her grandparents and they love her. She was the daughter they wished they'd had—good at school, respectful, a hard worker. She told them she wanted to be a doctor and they were ecstatic. A few years ago they moved to California for her grandpa's job, so she doesn't see them much anymore. Riley was given the option of moving to California with them, but she couldn't do that to her mom. She calls her grandad occasionally and he makes sure she is on the straight and narrow path to being a doctor.

In middle school, Riley used to stay at Mallory's for weeks at a time. She doesn't spend more than three nights in a row there anymore. She has to make sure Bella is on the straight and narrow path to making this month's rent.

Riley pulls up to Mallory's house and honks the horn. Mallory runs outside.

"Can I come in and say hi?" Riley asks.

"No, my dad is being an ass. Sorry." Riley knows what that means—Mallory got annoyed. *At least she has a dad who wants a relationship with her.*

"It's okay."

"We should skip our first period and get coffee," Mallory says.

Riley laughs and nods. Mallory looks happy enough this morning.

"Things with my mom are getting bad again. I think Brady broke up with her."

"Oh no, I'm sorry, Riley."

Bella does well when she has a boyfriend, but rarely do her relationships last longer than six months. It's gotten to the point where Riley feels relieved when her mom brings a new bum around.

"Can I crash at your place tonight? I'll go crazy if I'm in that house one more night this week."

Mallory looks at her with furrowed eyebrows. "I'm

sorry, Riley. I made plans with Jackson to stay at my house after the party. Do you want to have sushi with me, Camille, and my dad tonight before the game?"

"Sure. Do you think I could just crash on the couch?" Riley asks.

"Jackson's been down lately, and I just want to spend some alone time with him," she tells her.

"Okay," Riley says.

Mallory looks frustrated. "Don't be upset. I've had a terrible month. I just want to see Jackson tonight."

Riley misses being the one Mallory wanted to hang out with when she was having a terrible month.

"My gosh, you don't have to defend yourself. I'm your best friend; do what you want."

Mallory still looks annoyed, though. She always looks annoyed. It's hard to love Mallory. Riley has to tiptoe around the barbed wire Mallory has wrapped herself in. She has to walk ahead of her and pick up the glass so Mallory doesn't cut herself. Riley usually ends up cutting herself in the process. But she does love her. More than she's loved anyone. More than she loves her own mother. Riley loves Mallory's mom more than her own mother. Mallory is the only consistent thing Riley has in her life, even though she may be the least consistent person in the world.

Riley grabs Mallory's hand. "Why have you had a terrible month? Do you want to talk about it?" she asks gently.

Mallroy's eyes start to well up with tears. She shakes her head no, but continues to talk.

"I don't want to be here anymore."

There's something missing from Mallory's heart. Something Mallory will only find once she is dead. It's one of the reasons I love her. She's deep. She thinks deeply about this world that she so adamantly hates. If there is one thing Mallory likes, it's how much she hates life. You wouldn't know this from meeting her, of course. Mallory is kind, reserved, and charismatic. She's a fine student and a popular kid. Envied by every girl and chased by every boy. If you don't want to date her, you want to be her.

ELEVEN

The girls sit in silence at the coffee shop. They do this a lot. Riley likes to sit in silence with Mallory because it's better than small talk with fake friends who don't care about what she's saying.

"I'm sorry for snapping at you earlier," Mallory mutters.

"I know," Riley says, resting her head on Mallory's shoulder.

Riley can't pretend to understand the way Mallory's brain works against her body, so she is patient.

The smell of Jackson on Mallory's sweatshirt makes Riley feel warm. Growing up, he was one of Riley's very best friends. They went to everything together. He is still one of her friends. Platonic, of course, although Riley thinks platonic is a silly word. Platonic just means not romantic and romance is subjective. She would rather love a platonic soulmate than a loser she has romantic feelings for.

He still smells the same way he did when he was younger. His mom's high-end, all-natural laundry detergent. Their whole house smelled of it when she would go over there as a kid. Most moms probably wouldn't let their 8-year-old girl sleep over at a boys house whose parents she'd never met. But Riley had a "cool" mom. She misses the smell of their home. Jackson's parents treated her as their own. *Who wouldn't pity the poor girl whose mom is an alcoholic outcast who never went to her sports games?*

Mrs. Cooper went to her games with Jackson. She continued inviting her to family dinners once they got to high school, but things with Jackson were different. They weren't friends again until Mallory started dating him. But it wasn't the same. Riley doesn't think it will ever be the same. It took a while to get used to them dating, but she's learned that being the third wheel has its upsides. Now she can sit with Jackson instead of Blaire and Jamie at Mallory's volleyball games. Riley doesn't fit in with

Blaire and Jamie. She doesn't like them very much. But she does love them—in the way you love all your superficial high school friends. Riley thinks Mallory loves them a little more than she does.

Last week at lunch, everyone talked about not knowing how their own house smells because they've gotten used to it. Riley wondered what that would be like. She knows exactly how her apartment smells. She douses herself in perfume so it doesn't carry, but she thinks the smell is in her bones. She carries it with her no matter how many nights are spent sleeping on someone else's couch. Cheap vodka, her mom's cheap-smelling body spray, the smell of dirty men, and frozen waffles.

Before they leave the coffee shop, the barista slips his number to Mallory. Riley gets the same churning feeling in her stomach she gets every time a guy approaches her. When they are together, Riley becomes a ghost. She sees Mallory point to her and he shakes his head. She pretends not to notice, swallows her pride, and leaves without looking at him.

Riley thinks the boy who called her ugly in middle

school was right then. She wore cheap clothes and didn't know how to fix her hair. She's not ugly now. She knows she isn't ugly. But when standing next to Mallory, her features seem to blend in with the background. Mallory is the most beautiful person Riley knows. She has long golden hair that curls at the ends. She has big blue eyes and smooth fair skin. She's not too tall and not too short. Riley often finds herself imagining what it would be like to be that beautiful. That is the one thing she will never get used to about being best friends with Mallory. The feeling of invisibility that comes with it—even when she wears sweatpants and her boyfriend's sweatshirt.

They get to school just in time for second period physics with Mr. Cobalt. She sits with Mallory, Jackson, and Ethan. Half of the time they make fun of Mr. Cobalt and the other half they compare answers under the table. One kick means next question. Two kicks for A, three kicks for B, and so on. *Not a very effective system for cheating when no one knows the answers.*

Mallory goes straight to the bathroom before heading to class. Jackson doesn't even ask where she is. He looks off into space. Riley nudges him, but he doesn't say hi. Ethan gets the practice exam for the table. Riley waves her hand back and forth in front of Jackson's zoned-out face. He doesn't seem amused. Something's wrong.

"I'm breaking up with her," Jackson says suddenly.

"Oh," Riley's voice trails as her heart drops.

How dare he tell me that. How dare he burden me with this secret. How dare he break up with her and leave me to clean up the mess. We are supposed to clean up her messes together. That's how it goes.

"Maybe we'll start dating like my parents always joked about," he says.

Riley's cheeks turn red. She doesn't know why that made her angry, but it did.

"Excuse me?" Her skin is red as fire.

He tells her to loosen up and that he's just messing around. She knows he would never date her—she's not as brag-worthy as Mallory. She turns to face the teacher and feels her cheeks getting hotter.

Mallory comes in with puffy eyes. Riley can't tell if it's from the lack of sleep or if she's been crying. Mallory's face seems to brighten a bit when she sees Jackson.

"What'd I miss?" she whispers as if Riley was not worried about her.

"What's wrong?" Mallory asks Riley with her "you

91

are paranoid and stupid and I am fine" face.

But she is never fine, and I am never not worried. Behind every one of her smiles is a demon in her head, pulling her lips from ear to ear.

She watches Jackson and Mallory laugh with interlocked fingers as if their hands are not about to be pulled in opposite directions.

Jackson and Mallory walk with Ethan and Riley down to lunch. Riley keeps going back and forth on whether or not to tell Mallory what's coming.

At lunch, they sit at their table like usual. She feels out of place like usual. All the girls are skinny, blonde, and probably going to be checked into rehab before they are legally allowed to drink. Alcoholism isn't a word people use in high school. Instead, they say, "There is a difference between always needing to drink and always being down to drink." Riley wonders if that's what her mom used to say. *They will soon learn that when the parties go away, always being down to drink quickly becomes always needing to drink.*

The girls snicker as Genesis walks by. Mallory looks annoyed at the giggling. *Genesis is weird. I try not to pity her because pity is just judgment with another name. I can't help it with Genesis though. Her whole personality is not only annoying but a desperate cry for attention.*

"You're going to win homecoming queen this year," Genesis tells Mallory while stuffing her face.

Mallory humbly shakes her head. Everyone looks up at her with big, doll-like eyes. It's easy for Riley to remember why she's content to clean up Mallory's messes. She is followed by the crowd. Her life one big mesmerizing performance. When the curtains are drawn, and everyone leaves, Riley is the one who wipes her tears backstage. She doesn't mind it though, Mallory is her best friend.

Riley knows Mallory *will* win homecoming queen, even when she and Jackson break up. Boys always seem to come easy to her. And yet, Jackson is the only boy she has ever dated. The only one she let get close enough to know what else is in there. He found out and now he's packing his bags.

Mallory gets a call from Camille and runs out. Riley would love to go say hi to Camille, she's kind of her sister too, after all. But she stays because she's afraid of what the girls would say to Genesis without her or Mallory around. Blaire, Jamie, Ethan, and Caleb all sit and eat their food in silence. They give each other a look before getting up and leaving, claiming they are going to the library to "study." Riley hates them. She hates that they can't have one single conversation with Genesis without laughing.

Before leaving, Blaire points to the chain around

Genesis's neck.

"I love this. Where is it from?"

"The thrift store," Genesis says, turning red.

"Wow. Really fits you."

Genesis smiles and continues eating the rest of Mallory's lunch. Sometimes, Riley doesn't think Blaire and Jamie like her. They are nice to her, but they don't like that she is Mallory's first pick. They wish so badly they were Mallory that it looks like friendship, but it is not. They hate how un-boy-crazy she is. She's never been obsessed with male validation like they are, yet she gets it more than they do. Most girls take "keep your friends close, but your enemies closer" to an extreme. They make their disgust sound like a compliment and their judgment sound like advice. Mallory always makes it known that Riley is her friend first. She has a way of making people feel special. Riley never wonders if Mallory's compliments towards her are really insults. She doesn't think Genesis has had enough experience with female friendships to know Blaire's compliment to her was an insult. Riley talks to her and tries not to make it sound like she's talking to a wounded puppy.

"Did you know I take art with Ms. Penelope, too? I had her today for Intro to Painting," she tells Riley.

"That's awesome. I love Ms. Penelope. I've taken a

class of hers every year," Riley says.

"I know. You're very good. Today, she showed us one of your paintings in class as an example of shadowing."

Riley never knows how to take compliments, so she does the same awkward laugh she did when her dad saw her painting. She asks Genesis about her earrings. *They are just as hideous as the necklace.*

Mallory returns with coffee in hand, unsurprised that everyone has left. Riley thinks about Blaire "complimenting" Genesis on her necklace and gets angry, so naturally, she invites Genesis to Blaire's party tonight. Genesis seemed to appreciate the invite. If nothing else, it will make for a good story.

TWELVE

Riley sits in her math class watching the clock slowly tick by. Math feels especially long today with everything on her mind. She wishes it was Thursday so she could paint her racing thoughts away with Ms. Penelope.

Her math teacher asks her to stay after class.

"Your grades are slipping. Is there something I should be concerned about?" She asks.

My mother is drinking herself to death. My best friend should be evaluated and given meds. I'm forced to pick between two people I love. But the main thing is that I just really suck at math.

"I'm just having a hard time understanding the

material and falling behind on homework. I'll come in for tutoring after school on Tuesday to get back on track. I'm sorry," Riley says.

Her teacher nods, pleased with herself. Riley has always been good with adults. She was forced to be one when she was young. She knows what they like to hear.

On the way to the parking lot, Riley runs into Ms. Penelope.

"Riley! Have you opened the *Hallieanne* letter yet?"

Riley starts to smile and looks down. "Not yet."

"I know you are nervous, but you need to rip the band-aid off."

"I know."

Mallory looks like she's been crying when she gets to Riley's car.

"How was volleyball?" Riley asks.

"Good."

"Well let me drop you off. I need to finish my college applications."

Mallory starts chasing Riley like she does every time Riley says the word *college*. Thinking about the future stresses her out.

Riley can't stop thinking about what Jackson told her this morning. She knows Mallory won't take it well if she tells her, but she would be a bad friend if she didn't.

"Genesis better not wear that outfit she wore today to the party," Riley says.

"Maybe we should have told her it was a costume party. Anything but her normal wardrobe would be fine."

Riley punches Mallory in the shoulder but still laughs. Mallory turns the music up and rolls the windows down, sticking her head out of the window like she's the star of a coming-of-age movie. Riley apparently isn't doing a very good job hiding her inner conflict because Mallory asks her what's wrong.

She takes a deep breath and turns the music off. "If I tell you something you are going to hate, but I'm only telling you because I love you, are you going to get mad at me?"

"Of course not," Mallory says.

"Jackson's going to break up with you. Don't ask me how I know, but I am pretty sure he's going to do it soon. I know you love him. I'm so sorry." Riley places her hand on Mallory's shoulder, but she pushes her off. *Not a good sign.*

Riley knew Mallory would be angry, but figured she'd be mad at Jackson, not at her. Mallory claims this must be good news for Riley.

"This is stupid. Jackson and I are stronger than ever. Riley, he is not going to get with you. He never would. My gosh, are you ever *not* jealous of me?" Mallory raises her voice.

Riley knows Mallory doesn't mean a word she's saying. She knows Mallory doesn't think that Riley likes Jackson. But Riley starts crying anyway. Mallory is the one getting broken up with yet Riley's the one crying. They are sitting in front of the Bakersfield house now.

"Do you know how hard it is to be friends with you, Mallory?" Riley whispers.

"When will you see that you are not my friend? You are a parasite. I have to be nice to you. Where else would you sleep the next time your mom is too drunk to function?"

As if those words evaporate the tears right from her eyes, Riley stops crying. "Get out," she says softly.

Riley won't be going to sushi tonight. Mallory slams the door and runs inside. She knows Mallory will come and apologize in an hour and she will mean the apology. But the more Riley tells herself that, the more fake it feels. Mallory went too far this time. This fight feels different.

She has never called Riley a parasite and Riley has never demanded that she get out of her car. Riley has never demanded anything.

Riley starts driving home, but she doesn't want to be home. She doesn't want to smell the apartment. The car her father bought her is the only place she wants to be. She thinks about the word parasite. She wonders if that's what people think of her. A parasite to her father. A parasite to her grandparents. A parasite to her best friend. A parasite to Mallory's family. A parasite to Jackson's family. A pathetic parasitic charity case.

She stops at the fast food restaurant by the school to eat her feelings away. All the students come here. She turns up the music and eats in the car. Mallory is already blowing up her phone with apology texts. Riley starts typing but decides it would be parasite-like of her to forgive that quickly. She sees Blaire and some other cheerleaders walk into the restaurant. She puts her food in the paper bag and follows them in.

"Hey, Blaire."

"Riley! What's wrong? Are you okay?" She gets up to

hug Riley and pats the seat next to her.

Riley nods and says hi to the other girls at the table. She wishes it was Jamie who had an off campus study period and not Blaire. But it's better than no one. Riley has never once gone behind Mallory's back, so she doesn't know why she told Blaire what happened.

"Riley, I'm sorry. She's such a bitch! Please tell me you're still coming to the game and the party tonight. You deserve a night out."

Riley knows Mallory is not a bitch, but to be fair, what she said was pretty bitchy. "I don't know..." she says.

"Of course, you're coming. Let's figure out what we're going to wear."

Maybe Blaire isn't too bad.

As Riley pulls out of the parking lot, she sees Jackson's car pull out of the football stadium parking lot. Instead of turning left at the light, he turns right.

He's going to Mallory's.

To Riley's relief, her mom is not home yet. She tries to start her math homework but gets distracted by the unopened envelope next to her. The words *Hallieanne* in calligraphy won't leave her alone. She doesn't know why she even applied there—the top art school in the south. They only take 10% of applicants. Even if she does get in, she can't go. States away from her mom and from Mallory. Not only does she need them, but they need her. She throws the envelope in the trash bin by her door, opens her computer, and continues her application to Evergreen.

Her phone dings. It's Mallory again. Jackson broke up with her. She isn't going to the game. Riley knows Mallory needs her right now, but she can't stop hearing the word *parasite* every time she begins to reply.

Riley is studying when Bella gets home from work.

"Hey, Ry, how was school?"

"Hey, mom, it was okay. How was work?"

"Good. Are you going to the game tonight?"

Riley nods. "Can you do my makeup for the party?"

"Yes!" Bella says with much enthusiasm. "I would love to."

She lays on the bed and stretches out her legs.

"I finished my application to Evergreen," Riley says.

"No, don't go. I am going to miss you so much. You grew up so fast."

Riley laughs, and Bella puts her head on Riley's legs.

"I love you, Ry. I am so proud of you."

"I love you too, Mom."

"You look down, are you okay?" she asks.

"Mallory called me a parasite today."

Bella shoots up. Riley doesn't know if it was her protective-mother instincts kicking in or if she was just excited Riley was sharing about her life for once.

"She is just jealous of you, baby." Riley smiles and continues doing math. *That's a funny way to look at it. Mallory. Jealous of me. That couldn't be farther from the truth.*

When her mom gets up, she sees the letter in the trash can.

"You applied to Hallieanne?"

"Yeah. I didn't get in, though."

"They're missing out then. Why didn't you tell me you were applying there?" She asks, looking a little disappointed.

"You didn't ask."

"That doesn't mean I didn't want to know."

"Sorry," she says, flipping through her math textbook.

Since she doesn't have Mallory to sit with and all of her friends are on the cheerleading and football teams, Riley decides she'll get to the game as it's ending. She puts on her outfit for the party—jeans and a white crop top. After straightening her hair she's ready for her mom to do her makeup.

"Mom?" No response.

Riley walks out to the living room and sees her asleep on the couch. In front of her lies a poured-out makeup bag, ready to use, and a newly opened bottle of vodka. She switches the bottle with a cup of water again. Riley doesn't bother waking her up. She waits until she's done crying to put on a bit of mascara. She's never been good at makeup, even though she can paint well. But if her face is the canvas, Riley thinks the art has been doomed from the start. She tries to put on lipstick and blush but thinks she looks stupid. She sticks with chapstick and heads for the door.

THIRTEEN

Riley finds Blaire and Jamie outside the stadium and asks what restaurant they are eating at before the party. At dinner, she sits and listens to them talk about the game. They won. Jackson and Ethan made the winning touchdown. Riley wishes she had gone to watch Jackson play. He takes charge of the field like his life depends on it. She wonders how sushi with Mr. Bakersfield went. She wonders if Mallory knows they won. She pulls out her phone to text her but is interrupted.

"Riley, I love that you don't even need makeup to look pretty," Blaire's friend Holly says.

"Thanks." Riley stashes the insult, masked as a compliment, in the back of her brain to remind herself why she applied to *Hallieanne*. She can't wait to get as far away from these people as possible. Blaire, Jamie, and Riley leave early so they can change and get Blaire's house ready for the party. Riley sits on her bed and watches them paint their faces.

"Hey, do one of you guys want to do my makeup?" she asks.

They both look at each other and start squealing, arguing about who gets to do it. As always, Blaire gets her way. Riley watches her focus like she's performing surgery, putting every product on as if it were life-saving medication. Riley looks in the mirror at her mask. She looks pretty. She feels pretty. She feels like she could cry, but instead, she hugs Blaire.

People start trickling in and Blaire begins to pour drinks.

"Riley, do you want sparkling seltzer or lemonade seltzer?"

"I'm okay."

Blaire gives her a mischievous look.

"Let me rephrase the question. Do you want tequila or rum?"

All the girls stop talking and look at Riley.

"Blaire, don't force it if she doesn't want anything," Jamie says.

"Yeah, her mom is an alcoholic. This stuff is like the devil to her," Holly whispers loud enough for everyone to hear. Riley's face turns red. Blaire looks at her again.

"Are you sure you don't want anything?"

"I was going to say tequila," Riley says. The girls start cheering, and Blaire gives her a cup of something that tastes like rubbing alcohol. She drinks it all in one gulp.

"Woah, I didn't know you were such a party animal," one of the girls says.

Riley laughs. *It's in my blood.*

Blaire keeps giving her drinks. Riley assumed since her mom drinks more than a handle a week she'd easily be able to stomach all this alcohol. Before she knows it, the house is packed. Her brain starts to feel buzzy. Like a weight she didn't realize she was carrying lifts off of her. She doesn't feel like a parasite, she feels confident.

Everyone starts clapping and yelling. Riley turns to see Ethan and Jackson walk in. Jackson's eyes look happy. Much happier than they were in class today.

"Star plaaayyerrr," Riley says when Jackson heads to the kitchen.

"Are you drunk?" Jackson asks and throws her drink down the sink.

Riley rolls her eyes and skips back over to the girls who are talking about boys.

"I heard Jackson is single now," a girl she doesn't know says.

Riley nods. "In class today, Jackson made a joke about him and me being together." She doesn't know why she says that, but she knows she shouldn't have. She keeps rambling, because, for the first time in her life, she is the center of attention instead of Mallory.

Riley doesn't know how much time has passed, but at some point, Blaire calls her over to the kitchen and hands her another drink.

"Hey, Jackson wants to talk to you in the guest room upstairs."

Riley scrunches her eyebrows in curiosity and heads up. Time to do what she does best, comfort people when they are sad. She closes the door and feels like she's spinning. Like she could throw up or cry or dance. She settles for sitting on the floor. The door opens. It's Hunter, one of Jackson's teammates.

"Hey, Riley."

"Hi."

"Are you feeling okay? I saw you come up here."

"Yeah, I feel a little nauseous, though."

"Yeah, drinking does that. It's because alcohol makes our brains think we are hot so we feel sick. Taking off your shirt is always a good trick."

Hunter pulls her up and walks her to the bed.

Riley takes off her shirt and lays on her back. She thinks about Mallory. She thinks about her mother passed out on the couch. She thinks about the letter in the trash can. She thinks about her father. She thinks about how there is nothing she can do to fix anything. Her head is spinning. A wave of insignificance washes over her. She sits up.

"Nothing matters," she says with her head in her hands.

"Nothing matters," he repeats, nodding in satisfaction. "You look really pretty," he says. But he is not looking at her face; his eyes are on her chest.

Riley's cheeks turn red. She has never felt this feeling before. Boys never give her attention, so she doesn't know what to say.

"Blaire did my makeup."

"You should do it like that more often," he says.

The door opens. It's Jackson. He's shocked Hunter is up there with her. He tells Hunter to leave and asks her to put her shirt back on, refusing to look at her until she does. Riley tries explaining to him Hunter was trying to help her.

"Right..." Jackson laughs.

She's flattered Jackson thinks Hunter had other

intentions, explaining to him that guys never like her like that. When she asks him what he needs to talk to her about, he's confused. Blaire had told him she was sick and needed help. *Maybe Blaire is even more stupid drunk than she is sober.*

"How did the break up go?"

"It was actually okay. She didn't yell or anything. She accused me of breaking up with her because I was in love with you." They laugh, but Riley feels a burning in her throat. "I heard you got in a fight with her today," he says.

"Yeah. It's fine," she lies. She doesn't want to talk about Mallory right now. "She told me she thought I was in love with you." They laugh again.

"I thought I loved you in elementary school," he says.

"No way."

"Yes." Riley starts laughing so hard. She doesn't know why she thinks it's funny. He was genuinely her brother when they were younger. She tells him that, and he rolls his eyes. A few moments pass and Riley looks down to see his head lying on her lap. She starts playing with his hair the way people do in the movies. His hair isn't soft like she thought it would be. He has dandruff, and his scalp is dry. But she keeps running her hands through it.

"I miss being younger. I miss having you as my

brother."

"I'm sorry we stopped hanging out when you changed schools," he says.

"Me too."

"Remember Mr. Ricordo?" They burst out laughing again. Riley can't remember the last time she laughed this hard. She tells herself it's the drinks, but she used to laugh like this at his house. Riley feels her head pounding.

"I don't think I like drinking," she says.

"Is it true what you told me about Hunter? You have never done anything with a guy before?" Jackson asks. She nods. He seems shocked. *Does this mean he thinks guys like me?*

"Well, do you like Hunter?"

"No."

"Well, do you like me?"

"No."

"So you wouldn't feel anything if I kissed you?"

"No."

"Do you wish Mallory was here?"

"No," she lies. "Do you?"

"No."

"How drunk are you?"

"Not really," she lies.

As a little girl, Riley always thought Jackson would be

her first kiss. It just made sense. She doesn't realize she's saying this out loud. He looks down and kisses her. He looks dead behind his eyes. Like his soul has gone to sleep. His breath smells of beer, and his tongue tastes like nicotine. Riley keeps kissing him. Her shirt is off again. A few minutes ago he wouldn't even look at her until she had it on.

"You are so hot," he slurs. Riley knows there is no meaning behind his words.

She doesn't want him to stop, but she wishes this never happened. The door opens, and she shoots up in surprise. It is Genesis. *Damn it.* The realization of what she'd just done sets in. She starts sobbing. She throws her shirt on and runs after Genesis. She sees her car drive away. Riley stumbles outside and sits on the curb. She grabs her phone and starts calling Mallory over and over again. She has to apologize. She has to explain it means nothing.

No response.

Riley starts spam-calling her mom for a ride, but it goes straight to voicemail. Riley's reminded of how their relationship works—Bella is the one who's supposed to call Riley for a ride. Riley feels like a parasite in search of a ride home.

Camille!

"Hello?"

"Hey Riley, is everything okay?" Camille asks.

"No. I need you to drive me home."

"Grabbing my keys now. Send me your location."

Riley feels like the worst friend in the entire world. She knows Mallory would have never done this to her. No matter how much she drank or how mean Riley was, she would have never done this. *I thought she was undeserving of me, but maybe I am undeserving of her.*

Riley is crying with her face in her hands when Camille pulls up.

"Riley! What happened?" She peels her off the sidewalk and puts her in the car. Riley can't talk. She is crying too hard. "Did someone hurt you?" She shakes her head no. "Did you hurt someone else?" She nods.

Camille doesn't say anything but starts driving. She parks at a convenience store and runs inside. Riley rolls down the window and takes a few deep breaths while sprawled out on the passenger seat. Camille returns with two red raspberry slushies and hands Riley one.

"Thanks. I drank too much."

"It happens."

"I am just like my mom."

"Don't say that."

"I am. Did you know my dad was married with kids

when she slept with him?"

"Yes."

"My mom is a whore. I am just like her. I kissed Jackson."

Camille looks down. "You know Mallory has said and done some pretty awful things to you, too. She has a handful of issues, but one thing she is wonderful at is her ability to forgive. She knows you love her."

"Okay."

"Let's get you home. You can fix this in the morning."

Riley wobbles up the stairs. She wishes she had a sister like Camille. She can't stop thinking about Mallory. She feels stupid for what she's done to her. She can't stop thinking about Hunter. She feels stupid for taking off her shirt in front of him. She can't stop thinking about Blaire. She feels stupid for thinking she was a friend. She can't stop thinking about Jackson. She feels stupid for what they did. Riley opens the door and tiptoes inside. As silly as it sounds, she doesn't want her mom to see her drunk. She doesn't want to be a bad influence on her. Bella is nowhere to be found.

Riley goes to her room and sees a piece of paper on her bed. It's her letter from Hallieanne. Her mom must have opened it after she left. Riley reads the first sentence,

> **Riley Anderson,**
> I am delighted to inform you that the board of Hallieanne Institue of Higher Education for the Arts has elected to admit you into our university.

She pulls out her phone with shaking hands. She doesn't know who to call.

"Hello. Wallace? I mean, Dad?"

"Who's speaking?"

"Your daughter—uh Riley."

"Hello, Riley I didn't expect to get a call from you. Is everything okay." He is whispering.

"Yeah. Do you remember when you said you liked my painting?"

"No, remind me, please."

"Uh, it was a painting you saw in my room."

"Right of course. How could I forget." It sounds like he forgot.

"Well, I applied to Hallieanne, and I just got accepted."

"That's amazing. I'm sure your mom is very proud."

"Thank you."

They sit in silence for a few seconds before she hears the phone disconnect. Riley knows her grandpa would be so disappointed if she told him she's not going to be a doctor. She grabs the paper again and continues reading the letter. When she gets to the end, her heart drops.

> **We especially loved your portfolio piece on the alcoholic mother and her daughter. It really won us over. The emotion you are able to convey, along with your technique, is quite impressive.**

Her mom wasn't supposed to see that.

I am a terrible daughter.

I am a terrible friend.

I am a terrible human.

She passes out on the couch, right where her mom was this morning.

FOURTEEN

Lucas [loo-k*uh*s]:
bringer of light

Lucas begrudgingly rolls out of bed and drags himself to the bathroom.

"Lucas, I'm changing! Did you ever learn how to knock?" Mallory yells, slamming the door in his face.

"Stop talking to me like I'm a baby. Did you ever learn how to lock the door?"

They used to be very close, but now that she's in high school she'd rather hang out with her friends.

Lucas has a love-hate relationship with Fridays. He loves Harry's waffles but hates science class—especially on test days. He rummages through the pile of clean clothes he forgot to fold yesterday until he finds the vintage band t-shirt Mallory complimented last week. Before heading downstairs he hides the rest of his laundry in his closet. The smell of waffles makes his stomach grumble.

"I really don't want to take this test today. I'm going to bomb it," Lucas complains.

"Just do your best. Remember, we have the band banquet tonight," Juliet says.

"Don't remind me."

"Oh, stop, it'll be fun. Remember it's western themed."

Lucas rolls his eyes.

Mallory doesn't notice his shirt when she comes downstairs. He assumes it's because she is annoyed by Harry criticizing her outfit choice. Lucas feels bad for being rude in the bathroom and tells his dad to leave Mallory alone.

"You don't care when Lucas wears weird clothes," Mallory yells.

Lucas puts his head down and pretends not to hear. He laughs as Camille joins in yelling at everyone to stop yelling. He says bye as Mallory leaves without eating her waffles. She doesn't hear him. Lucas knows it disappoints Harry when she skips breakfast or refuses rides, so he asks Harry to take him to school.

Lucas's day crawls by as he anxiously anticipates the science test. After staying up all night studying, he falls asleep in first period English. He's scolded for falling asleep. The bell rings and he meanders across the hall to math.

He slumps into his seat next to Owen. He likes Owen even though he hates Owen's friends. In elementary school, he was friends with some of them, but over time they stopped including him.

"Look at what Mr. Guliver is wearing," Owen whispers.

They start smiling. His white button-down is so tight you can see his protruding stomach.

"I wonder when he's due," Lucas says under his breath.

Owen laughs.

"Owen, go to the office. This is the second time this week you've disrupted the class."

"Thank you, I was getting bored," Owen snaps back as he leaves. Lucas hides his chuckle by clearing his throat.

Lucas passes by the athlete's lunch table. His old friends don't even acknowledge him. Owen waves, and Brennan rolls his eyes.

"How much did his parents pay you to be nice to him?" Brennan asks Owen.

"Not as much as your parents pay me," Owen says.

Lucas starts laughing.

"Something funny, Bakersfield?" Brennan asks.

He puts his head down and walks to his table.

Lucas sits with his new friends from band. Harry helps Lucas practice his drums even though Lucas knows his dad would rather play catch.

Lucas likes his new friends, Dillon and Reid. He's never met anyone so determined to be different. All middle schoolers care about fitting in, but some people's version of fitting in is by not fitting in. Lucas is better at being different than being normal.

"What'd your mom send us today?" Dillon nudges his shoulder.

Everyone peers over the lunch table to see the four chocolate bars and a handwritten note. He passes the chocolate out to his friends.

"You have such a cool mom," Reid says, devouring his candy.

"Anyone sitting here?" Owen asks, pointing to the empty chair next to Lucas.

"No."

"My friends are assholes," He says, sitting down.

"Not as bad as Mr. Guliver," Lucas says. They laugh and tell Reid and Dillon about him being sent out of class.

"Sick shirt," Owen says before the boys head to their next class.

Lucas swallows his nerves and walks to science. He shares a table with Brennan—probably one of the reasons he's failing this class.

"The faggots back," Brennan says.

His friends snicker. Lucas truly doesn't care what they say about him, but he would prefer not to be in the room while they say it. He slips into his chair without a word. He drops his backpack in the process, spilling his things everywhere. His lunch box slides right to Brennan's feet.

"So sweet of you to give me food before the test, but I have to let you know, I don't like you like that," he grins.

Lucas prays the teacher will walk in as Brennan pulls

out the folded paper towel from his lunch box. He reads it out loud.

> Lucas,
> I hope you do well on your test, buddy.
> Remember to take deep breaths. I can't
> wait for the banquet tonight. I love you!
> —Mom

Everyone laughs. Even the girls. He's glad none of his new friends are here, but he wishes Owen had this class. He would know what to say to break the tension.

"Awe, are you gonna cry, Lucas?" Brennan taunts.

Lucas puts his head down. He wants to hit Brennan. But he's frozen. It takes him an eternity to gather his things before heading out the door. It's not a complete lie when he tells the nurse he feels sick. He calls his mom to pick him up. He's not going back.

On the way home, Juliet asks if he's okay. He nods his head.

"Do you think you could stop putting notes in my lunch? Moms don't really do that anymore," he asks nicely.

"Sure honey," she says.

By the time Lucas gets home, he's too angry to be sad. He shuts the door and grabs his gaming controller to drown out Juliet and Mallory yelling at each other.

Juliet comes in a bit later with red eyes. "Let's go say hi to Camille and buy you a new pair of cowboy boots for tonight."

Lucas groans but follows her to the car. He has nothing better to do.

Inside the boutique, he runs behind the counter and gives Camille a hug. He finds a pair of boots while Juliet gets sidetracked and tries on some clothes.

He sits with Camille behind the cash register. "Mom says you're sick,"

Lucas smiles.

"What did you tell her it was?"

"A headache." He laughs.

"Following in my footsteps, I see. I was the queen of skipping school."

Juliet comes back with a handful of clothes and talks to Camille about Mallory. Lucas pretends not to listen. They are worried about her.

Juliet pulls out her phone and smiles.

"Owen's mom just asked if you want to sleepover at his house tonight."

"Really? Can I please?"

"You said you were sick." She raises an eyebrow. "Rookie mistake," Camille says. "C'mon, Mom, just let him."

"Well, alright. I can drop you off after the banquet."

Lucas is packing an overnight bag when he hears Jackson's truck pulling away. He rushes out to see if he wants to play a round of video games, but is met by Mallory at the top of the stairs. Lucas follows her to her room.

"Did Mom ever leave you dumb notes in your lunch box?" Lucas asks.

Mallory nods.

"Did you ever get bullied for it?"

She shakes her head no.

"Oh. Well, I did."

Mallory squeezes his hand. "I'm so sorry, dude. That's the worst. Kick him where it hurts next time. Or better yet, let me deal with him."

He smiles and notices she's been crying. Juliet always tells him he needs to be better about "reading the room" and "noticing social cues." He remembers his mom and

Camille worried about Mallory. He suddenly feels bad for talking about his problems.

"Better yet we can have Jackson deal with him," he says, wanting to make her laugh.

She doesn't say anything and crawls into her bed.

"Was he here? I didn't see him come in."

"He's not going to be coming back anymore."

Lucas doesn't know what to say, so he hugs her. She starts crying more. Juliet is calling his name and telling him to start getting ready.

"Lucas, Mom and Dad think I'm leaving for Jackson's game after sushi. Please don't tell them I'm not. I just want to be alone."

Lucas nods. "Maybe he'll come back."

She shakes her head.

"He has to come back. He will miss you too much," Lucas says.

"He doesn't love me anymore. You are too young to understand Lucas."

"Well, I'm old enough to know that I love you."

She doesn't say anything. She rolls her eyes. He puts his head down and shuts the door.

She doesn't give me enough credit. I'm old enough to notice that even though Mallory is hard to love, everyone loves her. I'm old enough to notice that if Dad didn't have to feed us, he'd quit his job. I'm old enough to notice there's a reason Riley always sleeps on our couch. I'm old enough to notice Mom and Dad don't kiss anymore. I'm old enough to notice Mallory doesn't like living. I may not fully understand, but I'm old enough to notice.

Lucas changes into his western outfit.

"Looking sharp," Harry says when he comes downstairs.

Mom and Mallory are fighting again.

"Ready Lucas?" Juliet calls.

"Have fun tonight buddy," Harry says.

"I'll try."

Juliet was right. Lucas does have fun at the banquet. Juliet seems to love his new friends and gets along well with their moms. Lucas sits with Dillon and Reid, and they talk about the upcoming concert. Everyone is certain Lucas will get the main drum solo. He hopes so. Harry missed the last concert because he was working late.

I hope he can come to this one. Maybe Mallory will come this time because she won't have plans with Jackson.

On the way to Owen's, Juliet tells him he's a good

brother to Mallory and she'll need lots of love and patience.

"You're a good mom to her, too," Lucas says.

"Mallory will be okay. I'm sorry Jackson won't be coming around anymore," she says as he gets out of the car.

Owen and Lucas binge on junk food and movies until after midnight. Owen asks to start sitting with Lucas during lunch.

Most of the time, Lucas thinks having a sister like Mallory is hard. Worrying about her is all his parents have time for. But sometimes, it helps him out. He's glad his mom forgot to ask about his science test.

FIFTEEN

Camille [*kuh*-meel]:
perfect or *helper*

Camille wakes to music blaring. After telling Mallory to turn it down, she barely has time to get back in bed before she hears yelling downstairs. She presses her pillow around her ears. The muffled noise increases. These are the times she misses college.

She runs to the stairs. "Shut up!"

She stayed out late with Jason last night. She hoped he would make their relationship official at the karaoke bar but he didn't bring it up.

She's thankful to be out of the "getting up at 7:00 am

and being yelled at by her parents before school" age. Alt hough, she never fought with her parents like Mallory does. Camille is good at being a daughter. She made dumb mistakes like Mallory, but she was smarter about it.

Her parents didn't worry about her mental health like they do Mallory's. The dumb decisions she made were viewed as "normal high school behavior." But the dumb decisions Mallory makes are taken more seriously. Her stupid decisions are an attempt to self-medicate, not experiment. And, Camille cared what her parents thought of her; Mallory, not so much.

She doesn't know who she is, so how can she find the time to wonder who our parents think she is? I know Mallory better than anyone, but I still don't really know her. Or at least I don't understand her. It's hard to know someone who doesn't know themselves.

Camille sleeps another hour and a half before her alarm goes off at 9:00. She doesn't have to be up till 10:00, but she likes to spend an hour on her phone before getting out of bed. It sounds silly, but it isn't silly to Camille. She realizes it's probably a form of addiction. Her parents were right—it was the damn phones. Her generation laughed as children, hearing their problems were because of social media. They thought their parents didn't understand—how could they? They couldn't even work the devices they adamantly hated.

Camille used to say she was born in the wrong generation. But in reality, she is what she hates about it. She gets annoyed hanging with friends who spend the entire time on their phones. When she's with people, it is easy for her to put her phone away. It's when she is alone she finds herself glued to the screen. She doesn't like her own company—it's boring. It's gotten easier as she gets older, but she still finds herself waking up an hour early just to fry her brain cells.

Camille likes that Jason is never on his phone. She knows dating is hard to navigate in the age of technology. You think you owe others every minute of your day because they can access you at every minute. But Jason doesn't respond quickly. She used to think it meant he didn't like her but finally realized what he doesn't like is being tied to a screen.

She throws on some workout clothes and looks at herself in the mirror. Camille loves the ritual of getting ready. She loves the attention to detail—every skincare product meticulously applied, every unneeded eyebrow plucked, every eyelash coated in the perfect amount of mascara.

There is something feminine about being well-groomed. She hates that there is also something feminine about not eating. The act of criticizing her body makes her feel worthy of being a woman. No matter how much weight she tries to lose, or muscle she tries to gain. No matter the time she spends removing body hair, or the hair she straightens—she still feels the most feminine when looking at her distorted image in the mirror.

Camille is jealous of Mallory for two reasons. One, Mallory is beautiful without even trying. And two, Mallory doesn't obsess about looking beautiful. She just is.

She grabs her purse and heads downstairs. Her mom is cleaning the kitchen.

"Good morning," she says.

"Good morning, hon. I'm bringing Mallory by the boutique today to find a homecoming dress."

"Don't remind me I work today. I don't want to go," Camille groans.

"Just a few weeks before you start your real job."

"I know, can't wait," she lies.

Camille dreads starting her marketing job more than she dreads going to the boutique. She still doesn't know what she wants to do with her life. Over the last four years, she's been on five different career paths. Social media influencer, therapist, fashion designer, and teacher. Finally, she landed on marketing.

She doesn't even know what her marketing job will entail. She imagines it will consist of sitting behind a desk for eight hours a day. She's impulsive. She signs up for things that feel right in the moment. But when the time comes, there's always something else she'd rather do.

She looks at the other girls on their treadmills. They look like they belong. She rarely feels like she belongs anywhere. The friends she spends Monday with would be surprised that she goes to church on Sundays, and the girls that she goes to church with on Sundays would be shocked to see how she spends her Saturdays. She doesn't drink much. But when she does, she feels more bad than buzzed. She feels out of dress code everywhere she goes. Not enough skin showing at the gym, and (according to her parents) too much skin showing everywhere else. She always knows the right thing to say but often feels more wrong than right. A bad obsession with being good. Her mom says she's a natural-born leader, but most of the time she feels like a fraud. Too cursed by every mistake she's ever made to see the blessing she is to others. Worried that each mistake is an invitation for her siblings to do the same. And then she's worse than a bad person. She's a bad sister.

After the gym, she heads to the coffee shop. She orders two coffees. One for Mallory and one for Jason. She turns up the music and takes the long way to the school. She loves to drive. Mallory gets in trouble for sneaking out to see her boyfriend. Camille used to get in trouble for sneaking out to drive around listening to sad music. Not because she's depressed, but because she likes the mystery of moonlight, the enchantment of music, and the magic of the wind in her face. She calls Mallory when she gets to the school and asks her to let her in.

"Awe thank you Camille. Guess what? I got nominated for homecoming queen!" Mallory says.

"I'm not surprised. Can't wait to see your dress."

"Since when do you drink coffee?" Mallory asks.

Camille's face turns red and she laughs it off.

"Remind me where the bathroom is?"

She feels bad lying about Jason, but she doesn't want to get Mallory's hopes up until it's official.

Camille knocks on Jason's office door. He smiles and lets her in.

"Hey, pretty girl."

She blushes and hands him his coffee.

"This is a surprise," he says, clearly happy to see her.

"Well, I thought you might need some caffeine for your headache."

"Thank you. I definitely had a few more beers than I should've."

"Made for a great concert. When do I get to hear your next one?"

"Never." He laughs.

Jason pulls the blinds down. Camille sits on his desk with her feet dangling over the edge. He puts his hands on her waist and kisses her softly. He draws back smiling, gazing into her eyes. She runs her fingers through his hair and pulls him in for another kiss.

"We shouldn't do this here. I'm going to get fired," he says, grinning. Camille tells him to hush and kisses him again.

"I made reservations for us tonight. Marlo's Steakhouse at 6:00."

"You did? I can't wait. I've missed you all morning."

"I saw you yesterday," he laughs.

"I know," she says, tracing his face with her fingers.

"I have volleyball with Mallory in a few minutes. You should probably head out," he says.

"Already?" Camille asks.

He nods and holds her hand as he walks her to the door. Every time she sees him, time flies.

Camille really likes Jason. She says that about every guy she talks to, but this feels different. This *is* different.

SIXTEEN

On her way to work, Camille gets a text from Jason. Just seeing his name pop up makes her heart skip a beat.

Thank you for the coffee. Can't wait to see you tonight.

Camille calls Harry.

"Hey, Camille, now's not a great time."

Harry works too much for his family's liking and not enough for his boses.

"I was going to ask if I could grab dinner with you another night. Jason wants to take me out and I think he's going to ask to make us official," she says

"That's awesome. I really like Jason. Have fun tonight. I have to run."

Camille's never gotten her dads approval on the guys she dates. It's hard to win his approval. But Harry likes Jason and this makes Camille like him even more.

Her shift is only four hours today, but all her shifts feel like forever as she sits behind the counter scrolling on her phone between customers. Although, she'd rather do this than the marketing job she's starting soon. The boutique job feels temporary, but a desk job feels permanent.

Lucas runs behind the counter and gives her a hug.

"Where's Mallory?" Camille asks Juliet.

"She changed her mind. Lucas, go look at those boots over there."

"Did Lucas get 'sick' again?" Camille asks.

Juliet nods. "Camille, I'm worried about Mallory, she's getting bad again."

Camille takes a deep breath. "She'll be okay, Mom. Just keep loving her."

Juliet nods.

"I saw Jason this morning."

"Awe. Mallory still doesn't know?"

Camille shakes her head. "He made reservations at Marlo's for tonight. I think he's going to make it official."

"I'm so happy for you. He's such a good guy. It's about time you bring home a good guy."

"I know," Camille laughs.

Lucas comes back with boots in hand while Juliet tries on clothes.

"You don't look very sick to me." Camille smirks. "Following in my footsteps I see."

Lucas laughs.

Once they leave, the only thing getting Camille through the end of her shift is the anticipation of tonight.

She quickly says hi to Harry before running upstairs to get ready. He looks tired today.

Mallory walks into Camille's room.

"Do I look fat?" Camille asks, looking at herself in the mirror.

"No, you look beautiful," Mallory says. Camille changes anyway.

Some people wear oversized clothing because they are insecure about their bodies. Camille wears skin-tight clothing because she's insecure about hers. If people are distracted by her cleavage, maybe they won't notice her stomach.

"Where are you going?" Mallory asks.

"Another date."

Camille almost tells Mallory about Jason but gets nervous. She's pretty sure she'll be happy, but you never really know with Mallory.

Jason picks her up with a bouquet of flowers.

"You look beautiful," he says, opening the car door for her.

"How was your day?" She asks, taking hold of his hand.

Camille loves talking to Jason. He's a deep soul in a shallow world.

At the restaurant, the waitress tells them they are a beautiful couple while she sets down their food.

"Camille," Jason whispers.

Camille looks up with a mouth full of pasta.

"Do you know why I enjoy spending time with you?"

Camille looks down at her plate to hide her smile.

"It's easy to find beautiful girls. But your beauty doesn't stop at the surface. I like spending time with your beautiful mind. I like spending time with your beautiful heart. You are the most beautiful girl I have ever met in my life." Camille feels tears welling up in her eyes. "I want a future with you. I want to fall in love with you. I *am* falling in love with you."

"I'm falling in love with you, too," she says, unable to hold back her tears.

She tries to finish her dinner but her stomach is too full of butterflies. Camille is sad the evening is already over as they drive home. He kisses her in front of her house, and she feels at peace. Like she really could love him. Like maybe she already does.

"How do you think Mallory will react when she finds out you're my girlfriend?" he teases.

"I don't know. I am going to tell her when I get inside."

"Tell her I can't wait for the first volleyball game tomorrow," he says.

Camille smiles and shuts the door.

She rushes inside to share the news with Harry who is watching TV on the couch.

Mallory is waiting in Camille's room when she gets upstairs.

"Jackson broke up with me."

Camille drops her purse. "What happened?"

"Riley told me he was going to break up with me. I got mad. I said awful things. I don't think she will forgive me this time. Then she ended up being right. He said he didn't love me anymore. I was too much. I was too sad."

Camille's heart sinks. She sits down on her bed and begins the high school breakup lecture she's given her friends countless times. Mallory explains what Camille already knows—that her heart is breaking all the time. Camille learned at a young age how painful it is to be a sister. When her parents held Mallory in their hands, joy filled the hospital room. But all Camille could focus on were Mallory's tears. She felt them like they were her own. Everyone asked to hold Mallory. They said she had the most beautiful blue eyes. But when Camille looked at Mallory, all she saw was the sadness behind them.

She tells Mallory to go to the party.

"No stupid boy should stop you from having fun," she says, offering to do her makeup.

She's curling her hair when Mallory asks about the mystery man.

Camille takes a deep breath. "Coach Jason and I are dating!"

Mallory starts laughing and then her face turns stone cold.

"Volleyball is the one thing that's mine. You just had to make it yours. You don't think of anyone but yourself." Mallory yells, rambling on about how this will be,

" just another two-week-long relationship."

Camille's tears turn to anger.

I am always thinking about others. I'm never thinking about myself.

"Say something!" Mallory yells.

Camille reminds herself of Juliet's words at the boutique—Mallory isn't doing well. Camille tries to hug her, but Mallory pushes her away. For the first time in Camille's life, she doesn't know what to say to someone who is hurting.

"I have always lived in your shadow. Everything you did was better. Sports was the one thing I had. You couldn't live with that, could you?" Mallory screams.

Camille gives up on trying to comfort her. Her own words begin to move faster than her brain can process.

"Just because you are so miserable does not mean I have to be. You know you *can* be happy for people. Other people have problems too. You wouldn't know about any of them because you don't ask. Why should I feel guilty about you living in my shadow? I never put you there. You did that yourself. Maybe this is why Jackson and Riley are done with you. Take off my clothes and leave."

Mallory leaves without a word. Camille wipes the smudged mascara from her face.

Sisterhood is bearing half of her heart in your body.

Having a sister is like looking into a mirror. Your goodness and imperfections on full display. When one hurts the other, it is a form of self-harm. You stand with her scars on your body.

Camille sits on her bed and does what she does best: scrolls on her phone.

Her phone rings. It's Riley. She's in trouble. Without hesitation, Camille grabs her keys and heads downstairs. She smells her dad's cooking from the living room. Harry is sitting alone at the table. She grabs a bite before running out the door. She will never get tired of his cooking.

Riley is crying on the curb when Camille pulls up to the address.

"What happened?" Camille asks, peeling her off the concrete.

She's crying too much for Camille to make out what she's saying. She tells her to take deep breaths while she parks at the convenience store for a slushie. She gets one for Jason, too.

"I'm just like my mother," Riley whispers.

Camille shakes her head. They couldn't be more

different.

"I kissed Jackson tonight," Riley says between sips.

Camille pauses for a moment.

She is very drunk. She never drinks. This is not like Riley. Riley is a good friend to Mallory, a far better friend to Mallory than Mallory is to her.

"You know she's said and done some pretty awful things to you, too. Mallory has a handful of issues, but one thing she is wonderful at is her ability to forgive. She knows that you love her," Camille says. "You need to sleep this off. Come back and face it in the morning."

Camille punches in the code and drives through the gated metal fence surrounding Riley's apartment complex. She makes sure Riley gets inside before driving to Jason's. She can't stop thinking about Mallory.

She knocks on the door with slushie in hand. He lets her in with a big smile.

"Two surprises in one day. Lucky me." He grabs the drink and lets her inside.

"I'm so sorry Mallory didn't take the news well," he says.

She starts crying as he holds her in his arms on the couch.

"We'll figure it out. You're an amazing sister," he whispers, rubbing her back.

"If you say so. Do you think I could just sleep here? I really don't want to be home."

"I'd love nothing more."

Jason turns on a movie. Camille feels safe in his arms. Like he's taking care of her. She has spent so much of her life taking care of others and now it's her being taken care of.

"Jason…"

"Yes."

"I really don't want to start that marketing job in the winter."

"Then tell them you are going in a different direction. We can figure it out together." He squeezes her hand.

"I can't quit. I promised my parents this would be for real."

"Camille, you have to stop trying to please everyone else. What about you? What do you want to do?"

"I don't know. But not that."

"Then you have your answer."

Jason helps Camille send an email.

"I have no idea what I want to do in life. But I know

I want you in it. It's the only thing I've ever been certain of," Camille says.

She starts to feel guilty that she's not taking care of Mallory. But *she* wants to be the one taken care of tonight. Even if it's just until the morning.

SEVENTEEN

Jackson [jack-s*uh*n]:
son of the glorious one.

———————————◆———————————

Jackson wakes up exhausted.

Last night, he officially decided to break up with Mallory. He'd been considering it for a while. She hates herself more than she loves him. She hates herself so much he's started to hate her, too.

He drags himself downstairs.

"Good morning." His dad pats him on the back.

Even when Erick's being nice, he sounds mad. Jackson likes to think he speaks calmly, but sometimes he hears his dad's aggression come out of his own mouth.

"Drink up. Big day today," Erick bellows, handing

Jackson a protein shake.

"Thanks."

Today is the big rival football game, and the scouts are coming. Jackson would say this is the biggest, most important day of his life, but truthfully, it's the most important day of his dad's life. The only thing better than making it to the professional leagues yourself would be your son making it there, too.

Jackson's mom and sister, Kinsey, are at the table eating breakfast and talking. They look like clones of each other. Skinny and beautiful with long dark hair. Sipping coffee in their name-brand outfits.

"Good morning, Jackson," they say in unison.

Jackson looks like his dad. Tall, dark, and, as his coaches say, "built for football." It makes him angry how perfect his family is. There is no room for error. Ever. His sister is expected to have perfect grades. They are content with Jackson doing the bare minimum to be able to play ball. That's all his dad seems to care about. And his Mom just goes along with what his dad cares about.

Usually, in the movies, when an overbearing dad wants their son to follow in their athletic footsteps, the boy turns out to be a closeted theater kid. It always ends with the dad accepting his son's aspirations by giving a standing ovation on opening night. Unlike Hollywood,

Erick would never be okay with his only son starring on Broadway. And luckily for his dad, Jackson would rather go blind than dance on stage.

After winning the Evergreen football scholarship, Erick decided he'd play professionally. So he did. After getting any girl he wanted, he decided he'd win Jackson's mom. So he did. After he and Leah got married, he decided he wanted a son exactly like him. So Jackson was born to win. From outside the picket fence, their family is the epitome of the American dream. From the inside, it's less dreamy.

Jackson has an off-campus first period on Tuesdays and Thursdays, but today is Friday. He's not a morning person, but he doesn't mind his first class. History with Coach Jason. He's the cheerleaders' favorite teacher, even though he teaches their least favorite subject. He's Jackson's favorite teacher, too. Well, other than, the hot english teacher, Miss Lorelei. She's the football team's favorite teacher, even though she teaches their least favorite subject.

Jackson taps his foot on the ground and looks at the

clock for most of the class. He has to play well at the game tonight, but what if he doesn't? He doesn't want to break up with Mallory, but he has to. He needs to be a good boyfriend to Mallory today. He needs to leave her with a good memory of him. He has to make sure she doesn't hate him in case he changes his mind. He doesn't know when he'll do it, but he knows he needs to wait until the nerves from the game subside. Maybe after the game tonight. Or maybe after her volleyball game tomorrow.

One last day with her cheering from the stands. One last party together being the perfect couple. One last night of having a hot girlfriend to show off. One last morning watching her put my sweatshirt back on before sneaking out of her house.

Jackson knows Mallory. There will be no staying friends. The more a girl loves you, the more they will hate you when you stop loving them. She loves him the way Juliet loved Romeo, and he loves her the way he loves football. He didn't start dating her because he wanted to fall in love. He just wanted a girlfriend. But he did fall in love.

She's a good girlfriend. But Jackson doesn't think he's a good enough boyfriend for her. She is needy. In the beginning, he liked feeling needed. Recently, it's just gotten annoying. They both get angry. He gets his anger from his father. She was born with hers. He gets angry the way all teenagers get angry. She gets angry because she's not well. Mallory swears no one understands her—Jackson certainly doesn't. The part of her she polishes and puts out to the world, he understands very well. He liked *that* girl so much that he dated her. Eventually Jackson realized you can't separate her polished parts from her sickness.

When they first started dating, he didn't know how serious they would become. She was pretty. She was kind. She was fun. So it seemed worth the work to get her clothes off and get big hugs after football games. He didn't know how much he would enjoy her company and the intimacy they shared. A part of him doesn't want to let that go. But he knows he has to. Her neediness is too much for him to bear.

Jackson rarely uses his popularity to get things, but he knows the cheerleaders who sit behind him will do whatever he wants. He puts on his charm and asks for today's answers.

Coach Jason asks Jackson to stay after class. He's worried he got caught copying the answers. Quarterbacks can't be cheaters. But he's not breaking too much of a sweat. He's good at talking his way out of things. To his surprise, Jason asks him about Mallory.

"Should I be worried?" he asks.

"Not more than you already are."

He's about to tell him he wants to break up with her but can't muster the words. Jason wishes him luck on tonight's game and sends him off.

He walks into physics and sits down at his table next to Ethan and Riley. Mallory's not here yet. He hopes she's okay. If he could make her okay, he might even stay with her. He doesn't let himself think about what she might do without him. He can't be responsible for her mental state or he'll end up forfeiting his own.

"Mallory's in the bathroom," Riley says. The sound of her name makes his stomach turn.

Riley and Jackson met in first grade when you could be friends with girls without it meaning anything. In middle school, Jackson had a crush on Riley. He wanted to play Legos with her and watch Star Wars. Maybe a kiss on the lips before her mom picked her up. Only long enough for it to be sweet, not sensual. He even thought he loved her, but it was just a childhood crush. Once he got to high school and saw what girls looked like there, he forgot about Riley. That is until he met Mallory.

When Jackson was younger he was more impressed with a girl's ability to throw a ball than her outward beauty. But now it's hard for him to separate a girl from her beauty. He assumes as he matures it will be easier to do so. Although, he sees the way his dad looks at other women when his mom isn't looking. Aside from his dad's athleticism, he hopes to be nothing like him. But it's hard for him to separate his gifts from his father's.

Riley waves her hand in front of his face.
"Hello?"
He turns to her.
"I'm breaking up with Mallory."
Shit. Why would I say that?

EIGHTEEN

Riley stares at Jackson, dumbfounded.

"Maybe we'll start dating like our parents always joked about," he says, trying to lighten the mood.

She doesn't find it funny. He looks over at Ethan hoping he'll laugh. But he's too focused on his phone to notice the awkward silence.

"Excuse me?"

"Joking, gosh," he says.

Jackson's surprised. He was obviously kidding. Thankfully, Mr. Cobalt starts the lesson.

Mallory comes back holding two coffees. She's just about the prettiest girl Jackson has ever seen. Doll-like blue eyes, full lips, and long, golden hair. She hands a tardy note to the teacher.

After putting her arms around Jackson's shoulders she takes a seat. He thanks her for the coffee, dreading how awkward this class will be next week sitting between Riley and Mallory. Mr. Cobalt was clear. No moving seats after the first week of school.

He takes hold of Mallory's hand. He wishes life was this simple—nothing to think about aside from her cold, dry fingers between his.

But that's not life. Life involves talking and fighting and crying. And she does the crying part too much. I can't keep up. That's the biggest difference between us. I live for tomorrow, while she dreads it. She has a hard life. Well, her life isn't particularly hard, but she has a hard time living.

Riley is silent the rest of class.

Jackson doesn't let go of Mallory's hand as they walk to their lunch table. He finishes his food and heads to the library for the student council meeting. He hates student council. But, his dad did it, so he has to do it.

His friends thought it would be funny to put his name on the ballot for president, even though he wasn't interested in running. His vice president, Sarah Webber, does all the work. He just has to show up. Sarah is so perfect it annoys him. He can't stand how she's always the first to raise her hand in every class. Sarah should've won president. Apparently, she and Mallory have some kind of history. It makes interacting with Sarah a little awkward.

Today's meeting is about the dance. He lets Sarah do most of the talking. After the meeting, he stays behind to help her stack chairs.

"How's your day been?" she asks.

"Good."

She predictably goes on a detailed rant about her classes even though he didn't ask.

"I had to meet with all my teachers because I am on vacation next weekend and don't want to fall behind. My dad just got a big promotion and is taking me to Mexico. I had a math test, and I hope I did well because I studied all night for it. I spilled water on my shirt, and it was still wet while I was giving my presentation..."

Jackson zones out. He knows more about Sarah than his girlfriend from her 3-minute monologue. He knows Mallory better than he knows himself, so either Sarah talks too much, or he doesn't really know himself. He knows what he likes. He knows what he hates. He knows what he wants to do. He knows who he likes to spend time with. But he doesn't know his purpose. Sometimes, he just wants to drop out of school and join the army. Have something to fight for. But then he remembers football. That's his purpose—to win.

Jackson heads to english, his least favorite hour of the day. He couldn't care less about persuasive essays and the meaning behind *The Odyssey* (which he hasn't read).

But at least the teacher is hot. As in, supermodel, hot. Tight skirts, sheer button-ups, glasses, and a bun held up with pencils. She looks too young to be a teacher. When I was a freshman, I could've sworn she and Coach Jason had something going on. But now that I'm in her class I've learned that is just how she talks to everyone—even her students.

Miss Lorelei starts passing back Monday's test that Jackson didn't study for. He's on the cusp of failing english. She winks as she places his test face down on his desk.

"No one look at the test scores yet, please. Place them in your backpacks. You can review them once you get home. Remember, anything below 70 can be retaken. Tutoring hours are Tuesday during lunch."

She speaks with soft breathy words dragged out

between exhales. The bell rings, and Jackson heads to the bathroom before fourth period football. He unfolds his test and sees an 85 written in red ink next to a smiley face. His face turns red.

There is no way I passed that test. Maybe she's just as bad at grading as I am at testing.

Caleb and Jackson are changing into their gym clothes.

"Nice pink shirt, Caleb. It matches your complexion. Did your mommy pick it out?" Jackson asks.

"Shut up. The ladies dig the pink." They laugh. "You still planning on breaking up with her?" Caleb asks.

"Yeah."

Caleb nods. "Genesis took your seat at lunch after you left. I think you're being replaced. Breath of fresh air."

They crack up.

Caleb is a good friend. He's the funniest person Jackson knows. Last week, they hazed some of the freshmen on the team and put itching powder in their underwear. His dad pretended to be mad, interrogating the team about who did it. But once they got home, he couldn't stop laughing. He knew it was them.

"Let's take 10, team," his dad calls out from the stands. Jackson and his teammates jog back toward the bench.

"I saw you and Mallory got nominated for homecoming court," Ethan says, punching his shoulder.

He clearly didn't pick up on anything in Science class.

"Yeah, it's whatever," Jackson says, pretending this isn't new information to him.

The boys start whistling. Jackson couldn't care less about being on homecoming court, especially with his mentally unstable, soon-to-be ex-girlfriend. To change the topic Caleb begins to make fun of the assistant coach's unusually high voice. But after the laughing dies down, Hunter brings it up again.

"I can't believe you're still dating her. Wait until she finds out how that started," Hunter snickers.

The boys give an uncomfortable chuckle. Before Jackson can think, he pushes Hunter to the ground.

Shit. Please get up. My dad is watching.

"Jackson! No son of mine is going to act like that. Today of all days. You are excused," Erick yells out from the bench.

"Dad, c'mon it was just friendly fire. Wasn't it

Hunter?"

Jackson looks down at Hunter with a pleading face.

"Yeah, for sure," he says, brushing himself off.

Hunter is a year below Jackson, and since Jackson's dad is the coach, he knew Hunter would play it cool. His dad looks him dead in the eyes. Jackson leaves and waits in the car.

NINETEEN

Mallory and Jackson have a pretty distasteful backstory. After Jackson scored one of the winning touchdowns last season, he felt on top of the world. His buddies threw a party.

"I bet I could do anything I put my mind to right now," Jackson gloated.

His teammates looked at each other and grinned.

"Is that a bet?" one of them called out.

Jackson shrugged, the alcohol in his gut brewing up a dangerous level of confidence.

"I bet you can't take the hottest girl in school to Lovers Lot."

Jackson smiled.

"Who are we talking about?" Jackson asked, weighing the options in his head. Although, he knew there was only one obvious answer.

"Mallory Bakersfield."

Mallory was known for two things. Her beauty and her innocence. Which, of course, made her even hotter.

Jackson shook on it. Ten bucks from each of the boys at the party if he could get her to kiss him.

"I'll give you 100 if you land that one. The only thing better than touching a beautiful girl is a beautiful girl no one else has touched," Hunter laughed.

Jackson rolled his eyes.

The next day he began sitting next to Mallory in math class. Truthfully, he would've taken any incentive to sit next to her.

He quickly won the bet. It was her idea to go to Lovers Lot in the end. But to be fair, he chose the Italian place next to the school on purpose. That wasn't his first time being there, but it was the most nervous he'd ever been. When they kissed, he forgot about the bet. He forgot about everything. He enjoyed talking to her in the car. She was more than just popular and pretty. There was actually a brain behind those piercing eyes. He knew not to be too handsy that night. Not if he wanted to do it again.

After their first kiss Jackson found himself wanting to

see her again. He felt wrong telling his teammates that he'd won the bet. But part of him wanted their praise. It was an unspoken rule that the team wouldn't talk about the bet anymore once they started dating.

That's why he pushed Hunter. She can't know it started out as a dare.

Erick gets in Jackson's car after practice is over.

"I'm sorry, Dad."

"I know, son. I forgive you. But please channel that anger and energy into your game tonight, instead of taking it out on your own teammates."

Jackson nods.

"You disappointed me in practice today. Your mind is somewhere else. Figure it out. Evergreen scouts are coming. Tonight is the most important night of your life."

"That's a lot of pressure, dad."

"Live up to it then," he says, patting Jackson's back.

"See you at home?"

"I have some work to take care of. I'll see you on the field at 6:00. Let's run some drills before the game."

Erick is allergic to being home.

Jackson knows his dad is right—he needs a clear head. He can't wait until after the game to break-up with Mallory. He texts her to ask if he can stop by on his way home.

Mallory is waiting on the curb. He feels a knot forming in his gut. She gets in the car and kisses him. He lets her kiss him. It was the same girl he kissed at Lovers Lot. But as she sits in his car, he sees her for what she is. A beautiful girl with a rotten sickness. It's catching. She holds his arm and rests her head on his shoulder.

"I've had such a bad day, Jackson."

He feels something tighten in his throat.

"I can't wait to see you play tonight. You're going to be amazing as always." She says and continues rambling about homecoming and the party tonight. "Riley and I got into a big argument. She said the weirdest thing today. She thinks you are going to break up with me."

Jackson doesn't say anything. She looks at him, but he can't look at her. She pulls her hand away. He wants her to put it back.

"Oh my gosh. You *are* going to break up with me," she says, fighting back tears.

"I just can't do it anymore."

"Do what?" Her voice is breaking.

"This."

A moment of thick silence fills the car.

"I'm not happy anymore. I know my love for you is down there somewhere, but I'm only in high school. I shouldn't have to put this much energy into finding it. You deserve better. I can't love you the way you need," he says.

"You can. You do!"

"That's not true, and you know it."

More silence fills the car.

"You love Riley, don't you," she accuses.

He knows she doesn't mean that. He knows she wants to keep arguing so she doesn't have to say goodbye. Jackson shakes his head.

"Answer me." Her voice is breaking again.

"After all we have been through, I can't believe you would accuse me of that. You don't know me at all. Bye, Mallory."

She *does* know him—better than anyone. She knows that's not why he's breaking up with her. He knows her question about Riley isn't sincere.

"I'm sorry! Don't go," she pleads.

His patience is running thin, and he knows he's raising his voice louder than necessary. Just like his father.

"You can't beg for my love, Mallory! Look at you. You don't want to beg for someone's love. It's pathetic.

You just got too needy, too much, too sad. I can't love you the way you want me to."

He knows his words hurt her, but he can't take back the truth. She gets out and walks around the car. She opens the drivers side door and holds out her arms. Tears are running down her face. Jackson gets out and hugs her for a few seconds. He feels the knot in his throat grow.

"Look at me, Jackson. Look at me and tell me that you feel nothing," she says.

Jackson looks down at her wet eyes.

"I don't," he says with a straight face.

"I don't believe you," she replies.

"Even if I did, I can't." He is the one begging her now. "I don't have the energy to love you anymore."

Jackson hates that he has confirmed her biggest fear. She is too hard to love. Too sad to make someone happy.

"Can we stay friends?" he asks even though he knows the answer.

She laughs and shakes her head. He kisses her forehead before she leaves without another word.

Jackson drives home in silence. He's not sad. His mind is clear. He knows she will be okay. She just needs to take it one day at a time.

When Jackson gets home, his mom is packing for her girl's trip. She is always traveling with the other rich suburban stay-at-home moms. They love talking about their kids and loveless marriages while sipping mimosas on the beach.

"I just broke up with Mallory."

Leah looks up from her suitcase and pats her bed for him to sit down.

"I'm okay," he says.

"I know. You are always okay. But you know, sometimes, you have to feel things to get over them."

Jackson doesn't like being sad. His mom is the only person he can be sad around without feeling small. He doesn't like feeling vulnerable. It's easy to find anger and access it. But he's not angry. And he is not going to let himself be sad. He and Leah start talking about tonight's game. She follows him to his room and he starts getting ready.

"Your sister and I are leaving after your game. Let's grab dinner before we head to the airport."

Caleb picks him up to run drills.

"Pumped?" Jackson asks.

"I guess."

"What is with that attitude?"

"It just sucks being a senior that never gets any action. I want to contribute," he says.

Caleb is a receiver and a pretty good player, but Jackson wouldn't consider him one of the stars.

"You've had bad luck this season. If you stay open during the game, I'll find you," Jackson says.

Caleb shakes his head. "You probably should stick to what already works for this game."

"It will work," Jackson reassures him. "You are one of the quickest guys on the team. Just get open. You'll be fine."

Caleb nods.

"I broke up with her."

"I'm sorry dude. Hey, at least you won the bet. Does this mean I owe you ten bucks?" Caleb teases.

Jackson laughs.

His dad runs drills with some of the guys while

Jackson works with Caleb.

"Hunter, dude, I'm sorry for earlier. A lot was on my mind, and I didn't want that story to get out. Are we good?" Jackson asks.

"We're good, man." He says, putting his arm around Jackson's neck. "Let's go kick ass."

Jackson's dad comes to the locker room and starts giving a pep talk.

"...play like this is the last game of your life," he says.

Of course, he says that every week, so it's lost its effect. His dad always acts as if every moment is all or nothing. Jackson thinks sometimes, moments are just moments. But this moment is definitely all or nothing. Adrenaline is high and tension is thick as they walk onto the field. Jackson spots the scouts in the bleachers.

It's neck and neck throughout the game. Jackson really wants Caleb to make a play. He comes in for a few plays in the first half. Jackson looks for him every time, but he's only open once. He throws it cleanly, but Caleb misses. He's down on himself during halftime.

"You got this. The game is not over yet," Jackson assures him.

Nonetheless, Caleb sits on the bench during the third quarter. Finally, Coach puts him in for a play. They're down by 4 points with just 20 seconds left on the clock.

Jackson looks at Caleb as they break the huddle. He nods and calls an audible. The center snaps the ball. Jackson has never seen Caleb run so fast in his life. He takes off for the in-zone. It's not even close. Jackson launches the ball right into Caleb's hands, but the ball bounces out of them and into the air. His heart sinks. Just before it hits the ground, Caleb slides and catches it with inches to spare. The crowd erupts. They win.

Jackson played the best game of his life. Seeing Caleb catch that ball was the best Jackson's ever felt on a football field. He wants to do this for the rest of his life.

Jackson catches himself looking for Mallory in the stands. He doesn't think she'll be coming to see him anymore. The team begins cheering, hoisting Caleb into the air.

"Told you it would work," Jackson says to Caleb. "How do you feel?"

"Amazing. How do you feel?"

"Amazing," Jackson says. He means it.

Jackson is thankful he has Caleb.

"That's my boy," his dad says, giving him a hug. Jackson is taken aback. He doesn't remember the last time his dad hugged him. They find his mom and sister after the game. They're cheering, and his mom insists on turning the moment into a 10-minute photo shoot. For once,

Jackson doesn't mind. He feels like his parents are proud of him. He doesn't feel like that a lot.

Jackson picks his favorite restaurant. His dad has his arm around his mom while he says grace—Jackson doesn't remember the last time his dad prayed before dinner.

Kinsey and her dad start bickering about her boyfriend.

"Why does Jackson get to have a girlfriend, but I don't get to have a boyfriend?"

Jackson looks at his mom, "About that..."

"Oh shut up, you are ruining my argument," she whispers, and they all start laughing.

"Because I know how boys think," his dad says before grabbing his phone and excusing himself to the bathroom.

After dinner, his sister and mom head for the airport. Jackson is happy.

"Are you still staying at Caleb's house tonight?" His dad asks.

"If that's cool with you."

"Yeah, you go celebrate. Have fun. Don't be stupid."

Jackson's dad isn't dumb. He knows Jackson is going to a party like he does most Fridays, but doesn't ask questions.

TWENTY

"You excited?" Caleb asks as Jackson gets in his car.

"Very."

There are tons of cars in the street when they pull up to Blaire's house.

"By the way, I don't think you can stay over at my house tonight. I'm going to Jamie's," Caleb says.

"That's cool. I can get a ride from someone."

Dozens of people start chanting their names when they open the door. Jackson goes straight to the kitchen and takes a shot with Ethan and Hunter. He's relieved to see Mallory isn't there.

"You know the best way to get over a girl is to get

under a new one," Hunter says.

Jackson rolls his eyes. That's the last thing he wants to do right now. He may have just secured a college football career. He has real things to celebrate. Riley comes up to him from behind.

"Star plaaayyerrr," she slurs.

She's holding a cup in her hand. Jackson grabs it and looks inside.

"What's in here?"

"Oh, c'mon, chill out. I'm just tryna to have some fun."

Jackson dumps her drink in the sink and gives her a glass of water.

"This is not the place to test your limits with alcohol," he says.

She rolls her eyes and skips back over to Blaire and Jamie. Jackson heads to the backyard where he reenacts the last play with Caleb. He's five shots in when Blaire runs outside.

"Jackson, Riley is sick in the upstairs guest room. Can you get her to go to sleep or something? She's not listening to me."

Jackson rolls his eyes and stumbles upstairs.

She's sitting on the bed, with her shirt off, next to Hunter.

"Hunter. What the hell? Get out of here. She's drunk."

Hunter rolls his eyes and leaves.

"Why is your shirt off, Riley?" Jackson asks her, looking up at the ceiling.

"Hunter told me I'd feel better if I'm cold."

He scoffs.

"You can look now. I put it back on. He didn't do anything to me."

"He was going to," he says.

She laughs, "Well, that would be a first."

"Blaire said you don't feel good. Maybe you should go to sleep."

"What? I feel fine."

"Then why are you up here?"

"Because Blaire said you needed to talk to me."

Riley asks him about how the breakup went. Jackson tells her it went better than expected. He asks her about their fight. She blows it off.

"I don't think I like drinking," she tells him.

"Me either," Jackson lies.

"Then why do you do it?" she asks him.

"I don't know, it takes the edge off."

His head is lying on her thighs.

Her hands are in his hair.

"Have you really never kissed anyone?" he asks.

"No."

"So you like Hunter now or something?"

"No."

"So you like me or something?"

"No."

"So I could kiss you, and you wouldn't feel a thing?"

"Yup."

Jackson doesn't know what he's thinking. He's not thinking.

"How drunk are you on a scale of 1-10?" he asks.

"Solid 6," she lies.

Jackson lifts his head and looks at her. He doesn't think she's very pretty. He doesn't think she smells nice.

"Do you wish Mallory was here?" she asks.

"No." He's only half lying. "Do you?"

"No," she says.

He nods,

"I always thought you would be my first kiss. You know, in elementary school."

"Yeah, me too," he says.

Jackson grabs her face and kisses her. His head is spinning. Her lips are chapped and thin. He keeps kissing her. He slips off her shirt and lets his hands wander. If they had not been interrupted, he would've gone further.

Genesis is the last person he expects to walk through the bedroom door.

"Oh. Uh, sorry. Riley, is that you? Blaire told me you would be in here. Is Mallory here? Actually, I'm just going to leave."

This sobers him up quickly. Riley bursts into tears. He tries to calm her down, but she leaves and runs after Genesis. If Mallory finds out, he'll never forgive himself. He's so mad he can't move. He keeps imagining Mallory walking through that door like a sad goddess, but he wouldn't be able to comfort her this time because it would be him that she was mad at.

Jackson hears the door open again. It's Blaire. She walks over, sits next to him, and starts rubbing his shoulders.

"What do you want Blaire?" Jackson sighs.

She gets up and stands between his legs that are hanging off the bed.

"Don't worry. You will be okay," she whispers, leaning down to kiss his neck.

He pushes her off.

"Don't touch me," he says, standing up. "You're a terrible person."

She looks at him, smirking, and holds out his shirt.

"And you're any better?"

He grabs it and storms out. He can't find Caleb anywhere. He can't find Riley either. Everyone is looking at him. He walks outside, pulls out his phone, and manages to order a ride. He's fuming the entire way home.

How could I be so stupid? How could I be so careless? I need to make sure my feet are quiet so I don't wake up my dad. Damn it. I left my shirt in the car.

He quietly opens the door, but the TV is blaring. His dad must've fallen asleep on the couch. He looks up and finds himself staring dead into his father's eyes. Miss Lorelei is sitting next to him. Her face is bright red.

"I didn't know you were coming home. I was just talking to Miss Lorelei about your grades. You've been bombing all the homework. You're a mess. Where is your shirt? And to think I was proud of you tonight."

Jackson starts laughing uncontrollably.

He is criticizing me while another woman half his age sits in my mother's spot. Does he think I'm that dumb? A midnight student-teacher conference with a bottle of wine under dimmed lights. What a pig. Even with her lipstick around his big mouth, he looks like his insides. Mean and ugly.

Jackson walks to the stairs and pushes over a glass vase on the key table before heading up.

"Jackson Cooper, get back here and clean that up

right now."

"Go to hell, Dad."

Jackson slams his door.

He's overcome with anger. He starts throwing things. Then he begins to cry. He calls Caleb.

"Hey, what's up?"

Jackson doesn't say anything. He hangs up the phone.

He thinks about Miss Lorelei winking at him and giving him a good grade. He gets angrier. He thinks about his dad putting his arm around his mom at dinner. He gets angrier. He thinks about his dad saying he had work to do after practice. He gets angrier. He thinks about what he did to Mallory and Riley. He gets angrier.

I am no better than my father.

The anger in his blood and the liquor in his gut turn to vomit. He falls asleep on the bathroom floor.

TWENTY-ONE

Juliet [joo-lee-et]:
symbol of romantic tragedy

Juliet wakes up to the smell of waffles. She used to make a fuss about the sugar in them, but she's learned to pick her battles. She realizes most husbands don't wake up early to make breakfast for their families.

Harry's pitching a new project today. He's been up late working on it for a couple weeks. Juliet can tell it's important given he makes it a point not to bring work home.

She goes to the kitchen and sets the table for four knowing, like most Fridays, it will be a table for three. Lucas comes downstairs and gives her a hug. She holds on tight, knowing he will be too cool for hugs soon.

"How'd you sleep?" she asks.

"Good," he says. "I have a science test today, and I have to do good. I didn't do so well on the last one."

"Just try hard, Lucas. That's all that matters."

"Well, that and getting into a good college," he says.

"You're 13. You don't need to worry about getting into a good college yet. Right, Harry?"

Harry looks like he's in another world. She wonders what he thinks about when he escapes into his own mind, but she stopped asking a while ago. She never gets an answer.

"Do I have to go to the banquet tonight?" Lucas asks.

She'd never say it aloud, but she is dreading it more than Lucas. When Juliet was a young mom, she loved this kind of thing. But she no longer has the energy to pretend she cares about name-brand purses, interior design, pilates, or social status. She's thankful to live here but sometimes worries her children will catch the materialistic entitlement their neighborhood seems to carry.

Mallory runs downstairs refusing the waffles as Juliet expected. Juliet doesn't know why Harry keeps making them for her. Every week, she is "running late" to a class that she skips, and every week, a stack of heart-shaped waffles gets thrown in the trash. Every week, there is an argument about it.

"Mallory, it's hot outside," Harry says.

"And?"

"Drop the attitude; we are not doing this again," Juliet says sharply.

She doesn't know why or how, but they all start yelling. She hears her own voice coming out of Mallory's mouth.

A car honks outside.

"Does Riley want breakfast?" Juliet asks.

No response. Mallory runs out the door.

There is no disdain quite like the one between a mother and daughter. The mother sees what she used to be and the daughter dreads what she will become. Mallory acts as if I don't understand her. But I am very familiar with her depression. I gave birth to it. The umbilical cord is never fully cut between mothers and daughters. Whether she wants to be or not, a daughter is always a part of the mother's body. When one cries, the other feels it. When one pulls away, the other experiences immense pain. And so too will be the story of her daughters.

"Mom. Hello? Mom. Mom. Helloooo!" Lucas's voice wakes her from her thoughts. "Anyone there?" He taps her repeatedly on the shoulder and Harry laughs.

"Funny," she says.

"I'm leaving. Wish me luck on my science test," he

calls out from the living room.

"I'll keep both my fingers crossed, Lucas."

"Bye, honey," Harry says.

Juliet is cleaning the kitchen when Camille comes downstairs. She's thankful her daughter is home from college—there's less chaos when she's here.

"Good morning, hon," Juliet says, handing Camille the waffles Harry made.

"Mallory and I are stopping by the boutique to go dress shopping for the dance."

"Don't remind me I'm working today."

"Only a few weeks until your real job," Juliet says.

She's excited for her, but as Camille shuts the door she's hit with a feeling of loss. In the blink of an eye, all of her kids will be out of the house.

Juliet's day is a repetition of yesterday. Yesterday was a repetition of the day before and tomorrow will be no different. Send the kids off to school (though they don't need much help anymore), clean the house, go shopping, run errands, and welcome the kids home from school. Before she gets the chance to breathe it's time for band practice, volleyball games, homework help, teacher conferences, PTA meetings, and then the day is over. She loves being a mom. She loves the routine of caretaking—she finds joy in it. But that doesn't make it any less lonely. She wouldn't trade it for the world, but she would take a week's vacation if she could.

She gets a call around 1:00 from Lucas's school. He's in the nurse's office, refusing to return to class. Juliet sighs and grabs her keys.

When they get to the car, he asks her to stop writing him notes in his lunch. He says it with a smile. He clearly isn't trying to hurt her feelings, but he does. She didn't know this morning was the last time she'd ever write a lunch note for her children. Lucas's mysterious headache disappears after the 5-minute drive home.

When Mallory gets home from school, she storms past Juliet. Something's wrong.

"Honey, can you come down here for a second?" Juliet asks gently. She hears a sigh from the other room. "How was school?"

"Good," Mallory says, obviously lying.

"Are you ready for dress shopping? I heard from Camille that you and Jackson might be homecoming king and queen."

Mallory interrupts Juliet with a groan. She tells her she can't go shopping anymore. Juliet doesn't know why Mallory thinks she can just cancel their plans as if her life solely revolves around her kids.

She didn't go homecoming dress shopping with her mom either but that was because they had an estranged relationship. She would've killed to have had a mom to take her shopping.

Harry and Juliet went to the same high school as Mallory. They were crowned homecoming king and queen. She told her parents that night she was going to marry him. They laughed, but she was serious.

Growing up, Juliet never saw her parents kiss. They weren't in love. She swore she and Harry would be different. *They are different.* But it's not the same love they shared as high schoolers. It's a deeper love, but the fire is gone. She doesn't know how to get it back. She knows Harry loves her. But she wouldn't say he's in love. She feels guilty for wishing it was different when he is so good to her.

"I saw your grades today," Juliet says to Mallory.

"Cool,"

"No, not cool. You have two C's. You had all A's and B's last year. What happened?" Mallory rolls her eyes. "I'm speaking to you."

"I can hear mom. I had an awful day. Can you just get off my case for one second?"

"I thought you said your day was good."

"It wasn't."

"What happened?" Juliet's voice changes from scolding to soothing.

Mallory slams her door. Juliet lets herself cool off for a bit before opening Mallory's door.

"Get out!" Mallory yells.

Juliet sees her bleeding nail beds. She grabs her arms and drags her to the bathroom. She clips at her cuticles, applies ice and ointment, and paints her nails. Mallory's crying. Juliet wishes she could take off Mallory's pain and wear it herself.

"Thank you," Mallory whispers.

"What happened?"

She doesn't say anything.

"What's wrong, baby?"

"I was mean to Riley in the car."

"Well, that's okay honey. That's what happens between best friends. Apologize. She'll understand."

Juliet reminds herself to be patient.

That's motherhood, too. You put up with the ugly for moments like this.

"She thinks Jackon is breaking up with me today."

Juliet doesn't say anything. She just holds on to her tighter.

TWENTY-TWO

Juliet's phone rings.

"Dad?"

"Hey, hon. I have some news you may want to know. Your mother has been diagnosed with terminal cancer. Your brother just told me. We don't know how long she has."

Juliet doesn't know what to say. She doesn't cry. She feels sick. She hasn't spoken to her mother, Alissa, in years. Her mother left Juliet's father for another man when she was in high school. Juliet was so angry that she cut her off.

A few years later she swallowed her pride and agreed to meet for coffee. Alissa was shocked to hear Juliet was engaged to Harry from high school. She never liked Harry.

"Don't marry him. He has no money and no stable job."

"He has taken better care of me than you ever did," Juliet said. "This was stupid. I'm not taking marriage advice from a woman who left her family for another man. I don't know why I'm here."

Alissa left the coffee shop and they haven't talked since.

Juliet doesn't know what to say to her dad. She falls to her knees and prays.

I know I haven't prayed for my mom in a long time, but please give me time to mend my relationship with her before taking her away. Please.

Juliet wants to see Camille at the boutique even if Mallory doesn't want to come. She pulls Lucas away from his video games to buy him new shoes for tonight.

"Where's Mallory?" Camille asks as they walk inside.

"She isn't doing well. I'm worried about her. She started biting her nails again."

"She'll be okay, mom," Camille says.

Tears form in Juliet's eyes and Camille hugs her. This time Juliet's not crying about her sick child. She's crying about her sick mom. She doesn't tell Camille because she knows Lucas is eavesdropping. He's had a bad enough day.

Juliet gets a notification on her phone as she is trying on clothes. Her heart sinks. She braces herself for a text from her dad. It's Owen Johnson's mom—a kid in Lucas's grade. Owen wants Lucas to sleep over.

Lucas is beaming, begging to go. She reminds him he's supposed to be sick, but she caves as usual.

"I think Jason is going to make it official tonight!"

"That's wonderful. About time you bring home a decent guy."

Camille laughs.

Juliet is filling out the homecoming chaperone application when Harry comes home. He used to run inside and kiss her. He used to inhale deeply as if he'd been waiting for her scent all day. Then, it turned into long hugs. Then kisses on her forehead. Then smiles.

Every day she still waits at the table around 5:30. She puts on perfume and lipstick. She knows he loves her. But she also knows he loves his sister. She knows he loves watching baseball. She knows he loves grilling. She knows she is just something that he loves. And he's oftentimes too tired from work to show it.

She'd rather feel intimacy and live in a cardboard box than feel indifference and live in the suburbs. But it's not worth telling him again. She knows what he'll say. He'd hold her and tell her sorry. He'd mean it, too. Until the next day comes, and he's too tired to put in the effort.

Today, he comes in, drops his bags, and pulls up a chair next to her. He lays his head on her shoulder and breathes deeply. He tells her he's had a long day.

"Me too." She's about to tell him about her mother but is interrupted by the smell of alcohol.

"Have you been drinking?' she asks.

"I can't take the criticism right now," he says.

Juliet takes a deep breath. She wishes he would just tell her what's wrong. She leaves the kitchen and starts getting ready for the banquet.

Juliet feels guilty for not reaching out to her mother. She always intended to eventually. She always just assumed that one day it would get fixed. She tries to imagine how it would feel if Camille left and never spoke to her again.

How am I supposed to be sad about a stranger? I'm more sad about the fact that we are strangers than the fact that she's dying.

She reapplies her makeup. She doesn't recognize the woman in the mirror. Her hair is turning gray and her skin is starting to wrinkle. She used to be very pretty. She used to look exactly like Camille looks now. Juliet remembers hating the way she looked when she was Camille's age. How she wishes she could tell her she was beautiful. How she wishes Harry still told her she was beautiful.

Juliet walks into the kitchen. Harry is in the same spot. Every time she used to get ready for something, Harry would tell her how beautiful she looked. He doesn't even look anymore. Juliet goes upstairs to say bye to Mallory.

She knocks. No response. She opens the door.

"Hi, sweetie. Just wanted to say bye."

Juliet notices mascara running down Mallory's face. She knows that look. Her baby is heartbroken.

"Oh, honey. I am so sorry." Juliet kisses her forehead. "Do you want me to stay in tonight?" Mallory shakes her head. "Hang in there. I'll be back soon. I love you."

"Why?" Mallory asks.

"Because you are my daughter," Juliet reassures.

"You don't like me, though."

This is true. I don't like my daughter, at least not right now. I love her, but I don't like when she gets like this.

"I do like you. I love you."

"You resent me. I make you a bad mom because moms aren't supposed to have a hard time loving their kids. You don't know how to help me, and you feel like a bad mom. That is why you look at me and lie in my face when you tell me you like me. You feel guilty because it was your body that gave me these chemicals in my brain. And you don't know how to take them away."

Juliet starts to cry. "You are right about one thing, I don't know how to help you."

"Well, you can start by leaving me alone."

Juliet shuts the door.

Her tears continue to fall as she walks downstairs and grabs her keys. Harry starts asking Lucas about his day and Juliet shoots him a look.

"Jackson broke up with Mallory. Go talk to her," she says to Harry as they walk out the door.

Lucas is having fun with his friends at the banquet. But Juliet feels distant thinking about her distant mother. On the way home, she tells Lucas they need to give Mallory extra love and patience. She drops him off at Owen's and heads home. She realizes this is the first time she's been alone since getting the call. But she doesn't cry—she doesn't feel worthy of shedding tears.

Harry is half asleep when Juliet gets into bed. She takes a deep breath and asks him about work again.

"I have it figured out. Don't worry," he says.

"You always do," she smiles.

"You are the most beautiful woman I've ever seen."

She kisses him and rests her head on his chest. She thinks about her mother. She thinks about Mallory and the cruel things Mallory said to her. She knows Mallory wishes she could take them back. Juliet wonders if her mom wants to take back what she did to her and her father.

Dear God, Mallory isn't okay. I don't know how to help her. Please help her.

Harry holds her like he used to do and they fall asleep.

TWENTY-THREE

Mallory (mal-*uh*-ree):
unfortunate or *ill-fated*

I stare at the pills in my hand.

I think about slamming the door on my mom. I think about yelling at Jackson in the car. I think about telling Camille she's a bitch. I think about making Lucas get out of my room. I think about calling Riley a parasite. I think about my dad eating dinner alone.

My apathy has turned into rage. I am angry at Sarah. She told me this would work. Thinking of the people I love. It made it worse. I hate myself more. I hate myself for the way I love the people that I love. I still want to die.

I grab my phone and stare at the call button with

trembling fingers before pressing it. She picks up right away. Why did I call her? What do I say? The burning is hot. The noise is loud. My feet are dangling off the cliff. I clear my throat.

"Sarah?"

"Mallory? Is everything okay?"

I still get shocked when I hear her speak. Her voice is so damn gentle. It's so damn soft. She's so damn different.

"Why did you change your voice?" I ask.

"What?"

"Your voice. It's soft. It's not loud and sharp. You used to cut people with your words without even realizing it. Why did you change your voice?"

"You called me to ask, why I don't speak the same way I did in middle school?" she laughs.

"No." A few moments of silence go by. "You told me to think about the people I loved. You told me to remember my last moments with them. It doesn't work. You lied to me." I don't realize I am yelling at her.

"What?" she asks.

"You wanted to die and then you didn't. I asked you why and that's what you told me. *Think about the people I love*. It's terrible advice. Other people shouldn't be the reason I choose to live. It didn't work."

"Mallory, you never let me finish."

"No, *you* never finished."

"You had already made up your mind that whatever answer I would give wasn't good enough. You hated me for getting better so you would have hated what I had to say."

She's right. I hated her for getting better. I hated her for turning soft. I take a few deep breaths and remind myself she is not the reason I want to die. She didn't have to answer the phone. *She* is being soft, and *I* am cutting her with *my* words.

"Can you finish telling me? Please. Why did you not want to die anymore?"

"Every time I thought I wanted to die, I started thinking about the people who love me. I relived the last moments I had with them. The last interaction I would have left them with. That last interaction I had with them always made me feel undeserving of their love. It made me want to die more. So before I died I would go back to the people I loved. I would give them a moment I'd want them to remember."

I feel the hole in my chest deepen. I'm afraid I might fall in. "You never gave me a last moment with you. You were my very best friend. You just stopped reaching out."

There is silence on the other end.

"I'm sorry, Mallory. The best way I could love you

was to stop being your friend." I think she might be crying. "I can't talk you out of wanting to die. If you want to die, at least go back to the people you love and give them a moment to remember."

I can't take the pills. Not tonight. Not after how I left things. Tomorrow has to be perfect. I have to make things right before I die.

I stash the sleeping pills under my pillow.

TWENTY-FOUR

The sound of my alarm fills me with dread.

I can't let this dread take over. Not today. Not on the last day my family and friends have with me. I check and make sure the bottle is still under my pillow.

I drink coffee with Jason and Camille.

I hate to admit it, but I like them together.

I shop for a dress with my mom.

I hug her tight when she tells me about her mom.

I celebrate Riley's acceptance into *Hallieanne*.

I forgive her drunk actions. She forgives my sober words.

I eat sushi with my dad.

I told him he should be a chef after hearing about his job.

I make the winning spike at our first volleyball game.

I smile at Jackson after he cheers for me from the stands.

I toilet paper Brennan's house with Lucas.

I congratulate him on getting the big drum solo.

It was a *good* day.

I walk up to my room. I reach under my pillow. I open the bottle of pills. The burning is still hot. The noise is still loud. My feet are still dangling off the cliff. My heart is still aching. My demons are still dancing. But the pills are no longer begging to be consumed.

The pain is still there. But it is no longer alone.

TWENTY-FIVE

I don't think we can save others. I don't even think we can save ourselves. Thinking about the people who love me was never the answer. Knowing you are loved doesn't cure wanting to die. But I am starting to wonder if loving others might give me enough reason to stay alive.

It has certainly given the people in my life a reason to wake up every morning. Even when the person they love is mean and cruel and ditches dinner with her dad and calls her best friend a parasite and slams the door on her little brother and calls her sister a bitch and yells at her boyfriend and cancels shopping with her mom. They love her either way. Without condition.

I don't think I'll ever be cured of the imbalance in my

brain. Coach Jason said there is always a purpose in pain. I've spent my whole life searching for this purpose. Sometimes people are born with an obvious purpose. My dad was born to cook. Riley was born to paint. Lucas was born to play drums. Camille was born to help others. Jason was born to coach. Jackson was born to play ball. My mom was born to be a mom.

I've been so fixated on the fact that I was born without a purpose, I never stopped to consider that my pain might be my purpose. Something that gives me a deeper appreciation for the little things in life. Like eating dinner with my dad or seeing my best friend get into her dream school or watching my brother make new friends or seeing my sister fall in love or shopping with my mom.

Perhaps this sadness in me is proof of what Coach Jason said God is saving us from. Perhaps the act of loving proves what he is saving us for.

Riley thinks there is something missing from my heart—something I will only find once I'm dead. So maybe the answer is to live like I am going to be dead. Love others like I am going to be gone. It takes me out of my head. Out of the body I wanted to kill.

Loving because I was in their shoes, not just trying to escape from my own. Every moment an interaction I would want them to remember.

One more day.

And always one more day.

EPILOGUE

I stopped eating lunch with Blaire.

I sat with Riley, Sarah, and Genesis the rest of the year.

We've stayed close friends.

Jackson and I had a blast at homecoming.

We laughed as we were crowned king and queen.

My grandma passed away.

But not before sitting with Mom at my graduation.

Jackson became the *Evergreen* quarterback.

Riley went on to attend *Hallieanne*.

My dad opened his first restaurant. It was a huge success.

He hired the bartender he met that day he got fired.

Camille is the general manager of *Bakersfield Cafe*.

My mom fell in love with my dad all over again—

watching him fall in love with his craft.

Lucas and his new friends started a band.

They play at all of their high school events.

Owen has never missed a concert.

Jackson doesn't speak much to his dad anymore.

We keep in touch. He really *did* want to stay friends.

Riley's mom never got sober.

But she waited all year to take me to Riley's art gallery.

Her proud grandpa flew in from California.

Camille and Jason got married the following year.

Riley and I loved being bridesmaids.

I'm going to be an aunt soon.

I went on to help girls like me.

I found that helping others helps me too.

I was invited to be this year's speaker at my old middle school's suicide prevention assembly.

> "...I used to sit in those very seats. I walked away from this same assembly angry. Nothing that was said made me better. Whoever tells you that you're supposed to be happy is lying. Happiness is dependent on circumstances out of our control. It's never been about being happy. Life is about loving others. It is about loving others even

when you are sad, because real love isn't de-pendent on circumstances. And real love is a lot more meaningful than being happy will ever be. What's the purpose in taking death into your own hands? For death has lost its beauty if we do not first live, and life has lost its beauty if we do not first love..."

My name is Mallory.

Mallory means *unfortunate* or *ill-fated.*

The girl behind the picket fence took fate into her hands.

I found that my voice got softer along the way.

Author's Note
Why I Wrote This Book

I am an author. I am addicted to sadness.
They are one and the same.
You cannot have one without the other.

That was something I wrote a couple of years back. Something, up until fairly recently, I absolutely believed. My sadness has an ego—it longs to be turned into art.

There is a lie deeply ingrained in the creative world. *You must be sad to create good art.* This is something I had to unlearn. Especially while writing this novel. For if I let myself fall into the trenches of my own despair, how would I help the characters I write about overcome theirs?

This idea that, as a creative, the cards are stacked against me, plagued my mind for a long time. And the dark truth of the matter is the cards *are* stacked against me. If you look at almost every artist through out history, you see they often lived grim lives filled with suicidal ideations. Sylvia Plath, Amy Winehouse, Pablo Picasso, Robin Williams, William Shakespeare, and (my personal favorite) Vincent Van Gogh.

I cannot sit idly by and lose with my faulty hand just because that's what I've been given. Just as Mallory had to take her fate into her own hands, I must take a gamble on myself.

While there is no science linking creativity to sadness, they are often seen as intertwined. I think it's because creatives don't know how to create unless they are sad. And they don't know what to do when they are sad besides create. This cycle can drive a person insane.

While writing this book, I learned that one thing inspires people more than sadness: *hope*. You don't need to be sad to create good art. You just need to hope for something better.

I was born with the curse all creatives are burdened with. I loved life, yet I always had a ribbon of sadness running through my blood. Sad souls are often tormented by a desire to find purpose in their pain. It is only after you learn, sometimes your purpose is your pain, that you find peace. Sadness can be a gift, not for you, but for the people you love. Not so you can have an excuse to drown in your tears, but so you can be an example of triumph for others as you swim through the rapids. I've come to experience joy in my pain. Not happiness, for happiness is dependent on circumstances, but joy. Because not only have I found my love of writing through my pain, I have found peace in my pain.

In ancient Greek, sadness means *sobriety*. Those who are sad are too sober for this drunken world. Of course, creatives often have a reputation for being isolated pricks that drink themselves to death. One of my favorite authors, Stephen King, says it perfectly in his book, 'On Writing': *"The idea that creative endeavor and mind-altering substances are entwined is one of the great pop-intellectual myths of our time. Creative people probably do run a greater risk of alcoholism and addiction than those in some other jobs, but so what? We all look pretty much the same when we're puking in the gutter."*

In Latin, sadness means *fullness.* An emotion so overwhelming it takes absolute control. Sad souls are full of suffering, surrounded by those who empty themselves to not be sad.

The story of Job has always fascinated me. Job was described, in all respects, as a rich and noble man. He was regarded as one who did good to others. One day Satan approached God and asked for people to tempt and torment. God said to Satan, *"Have you considered my servant Job, there is none like him on the earth, a blameless and upright man, who fears God and turns away from evil?"* (Job 1:8, ESV)

This is as perplexing as a robber coming to a bank and the owner not only letting him in, but showing him to the most expensive vault containing silver coins and gold bars. Satan then challenged God, *"You have blessed the work of his hands, and his possessions have increased in the land. But stretch out your hand and touch all that he has, and he will curse you to your face."* (1:9-11). Satan was confident that if struck with the evils of this world, if stripped from all comfort he had, Job's trust in God would vanish. His faithfulness towards God would turn to anger towards God.

The Lord replied to Satan, *"Behold, all that he has is in your hand. Only against him do not stretch out your hand." (1:12).* He allowed Satan to destroy all that Job had, even allowing him to physically harm Job, as long as he spared his life. This verse changed the way I view suffering. When Satan destroys, it is with the knowledge and allowance of God. God draws the lines for Satan and tells him where he can and cannot go. Even though Satan may have dominion over the earth, his power is restricted and limited. Every time I go through pain or feel sadness, God has allowed that to take place. Satan cannot escape God's sovereignty. Job went on to lose all that he had and mourn his birth and very existence.

At the end of the story, Job asked God the question that many ask today. *If God is good, why is there suffering?* God responded in a peculiar way, by asking him a series of questions. *"Where were you when I laid the foundation of the earth?"* (38:4), *"Have you commanded the morning since your days began...?* (38:12), *"Can you... loose the chords of Orion?"* (38:31), *"Can you send forth light-nings...?"* (38:35), *"Can you hunt the prey for the lion...?"* (38:39), *"Do you know when the mountain goats give birth?"* (39:1)

God's response to Job is redirecting him to God's sovereignty—the very thing that allowed his suffering. Who is Job to ask the Creator of the universe why he allows things to happen? Instead of giving Job a reason for his pain, he assures him that there *is* a reason, as sure as the lions will get fed and the lightning will strike.

"And the Lord gave Job twice as much as he had before." (42:10). Though Job never asked God to restore all he had lost, God gave him all he had and more, *"And Job*

died, an old man, full of days." (42:17). How did Job die full of life after so much of it had been stripped from him? I imagine it was because he stopped questioning *why* sorrow existed and instead learned *how* to use his sorrow to mold him into a better man. For, how can a happy man know he is happy without ever feeling sad?

You can't eliminate sorrow by neglecting to feel it. You cannot eliminate sorrow by wallowing in it. Sorrow itself isn't a *good* feeling. But you can *find* goodness in it. Sorrow can help us reflect on the joys of life. I hope this book brought you as much joy to read as it gave me to write.

May your sadness teach you that you need saving.

May your sadness point to what God has saved us from.

May your sadness not make you want to end your life.

May your sadness be something you use
                              to appreciate life's beauty.

Acknowledgment

Thank you, David M., for the countless hours you spent copy editing this dyslexic author's book. Thank you, M.M. Jack Beetle, for always believing in me. Thank you to the brown couch where this book was written. Thank you to my late nana for helping me grow into the woman I am. Thank you to the Stites for giving me my best friend and my second home. Thank you to my father for being my number one supporter. Without your encouragement, this book would never have come to fruition. Thank you to my mother for passing down your love for words. Thank you for the sleep you sacrificed reading every version of this story—from a high school assignment, to a script, to a short story, to my first novel. And thank you *you*, my unknown reader, for your part in fulfilling my dreams.

KORI JANE SPAULDING grew up in Houston, Texas. As a rising voice in contemporary poetry, she garnered acclaim for her debut poetry collection, *Books Close*. Shortly after, she published her sequel poetry collection, *Open Wounds*. *Behind The Picket Fence* is her first novel.

Made in United States
Orlando, FL
14 December 2024

55483446R00138